We Both End Up With Scars

Tina J

Copyright 2020

This novel is a work of fiction. Any resemblances to actual events, real people, living or dead, organizations, establishments or locales are products of the author's imagination. Other names, characters, places, and incidents are used fictionally.

All parts reserved. No part of this book may be used or reproduced in any form or by any means electronic or mechanical, including photocopying, recording or by information storage and retrieval system, without written permission from the publisher and write.

Because of the dynamic nature of the Internet, any web address or links contained in this book may have changed since publication, and may no longer be valid.

<u>Warning:</u>

This book is strictly Urban Fiction and the story is <u>NOT</u> <u>REAL</u>!

Characters will not behave the way you want them to; nor will they react to situations the way you think they should. Some of them may be drug addicts, kingpins, savages, thugs, rich, poor, ho's, sluts, haters, bitter ex-girlfriends or boyfriends, people from the past and the list can go on and on. That is what Urban Fiction mostly consists of. If this isn't anything you foresee yourself interested in, then do yourself a favor and don't read it because it's only going to piss you off. ☺☺

Also, the book will not end the way you want so please be advised that the outcome will be based solely on my own thoughts and ideas. I hope you enjoy this book that y'all made me write. Thanks so much to my readers, supporters, publisher and fellow authors and authoress for the support. 😲😲

Author Tina J

Caught Up Loving A Beast 1, 2 & 3

A Street King And His Shawty 1 & 2

I Fell For The Wrong Bad Boy 1&2

I Wanna Love You 1 & 2

Addicted to Loving a Boss 1, 2, & 3

I Need That Gangsta Love 1&2

Creepin With The Plug 1 & 2

All Eyes On The Crown 1,2&3

When She's Bad, I'm Badder: Jiao and Dreek, A Crazy

Love Story 1,2&3

Still Luvin A Beast 1&2

Her Man, His Savage 1 & 2

Marco & Rakia: Not Your Ordinary, Hood Kinda Love 1,2

& 3

Feenin For A Real One 1, 2 & 3

A Kingpin's Dynasty 1, 2 & 3

What Kinda Love Is This: Captivating A Boss 1, 2 & 3

Frankie & Lexi: Luvin A Young Beast 1, 2 & 3

A Dope Boys Seduction 1, 2 & 3

My Brother's Keeper 1. 2 & 3

C'Yani & Meek: A Dangerous Hood Love 1, 2 & 3

When A Savage Falls for A Good Girl 1, 2 & 3

Eva & Deray 1 & 2

Blame It On His Gangsta Luv 1 & 2

Falling for The Wrong Hustla 1, 2 & 3

I Gave My Heart to A Jersey Killa 1, 2 & 3

Luvin The Son of a Savage 1, 2 & 3

A Dopeman and His Shawty 1, 2 & 3

Somebody Else's Thug 1, 2 & 3

Can't Trust Them Thugs 1, 2 & 3

Luvin' The Wrong Thug 1, 2& 3

<u>Cadence</u>

"Yo, this pussy is garbage. Haven't I taught you anything? Do you even listen when I speak? Get the fuck out my face." Tristan yelled and continued to degrade me, as I put my clothes back on.

I shut the door and listened to him continue fucking another chick in our bed. This was our normal Saturday nights, unless I was on my period; and even then, he felt like oral sex was a must. I had to get my life together, because this was not how I portrayed it to be.

I met Tristan four years ago, when I was a junior in high school. I had recently moved from Texas to New Jersey, so I was considered new meat. I was a bit of a loner being the new kid, until Tristan bumped into me by accident.

"Damn girl, I'm sorry about that." I bent down to pick my things up, and when I looked up, he was smiling.

Tristan was dark- skinned with dreads hanging down his back. His physique was immaculate, which came from him being on the football team. He had light brown eyes and a nice smile. I wouldn't say his teeth were perfect, but at least, they weren't butter yellow.

"That's ok. I should've been paying attention anyway." He passed me the pen that was left and walked off.

Every day after that, he started sitting with me in the lunchroom and inviting me to his games. People kept asking if we were a couple, but he would just tell them I was the front-runner in the race.

One day, he finally asked me to be his girl when we were sitting at his house watching a movie. Once I said yes, he immediately assumed we were going to have sex. Needless to say, that never happened. I still had my V card and planned on keeping it. He would give me oral sex, and it was ok, but I felt like it was too sloppy. I mean, when he finished, I was wiping up so much that I felt like he was slobbing more than anything. He graduated a year before me, and we were still dating.

The night of my senior prom, Tristan escorted me. He rented a room, and to say the night was magical, would be a lie. I was in love with him, so I decided to give him what he wanted, which was my virginity. Low and behold, it was nothing that I expected. There was no sparks; it wasn't pleasant, and it lasted a few minutes once he got in. He passed out right after.

The summer after I graduated, I enrolled in the local community college, because I wasn't ready to move out. I still lived with my mom and dad, and they told me to take my time trying to be grown. I didn't understand what they meant in the beginning, but four years later; and living with a no good nigga whose idea of good sex was inviting other chicks in our bedroom, is not how I imagined my life. The message was received loud and clear now.

****

I walked in the living room, sat on the couch, and turned the TV up to distract me from the bed squeaking. The door opened an hour later, and he came out with Bambi, kissing. I sucked my teeth and rolled my eyes as he walked her out. I saw her getting in a blue mustang, and he handed her off some money. He walked back in, shut the door and sat next to me on the couch smelling like fish.

"Yo' get your ass in here." He screamed, causing me to jump. I walked out the bathroom dry heaving as he sat there ignoring the stench. I pulled the shirt up over my nose.

"Cady, we have to talk." Cady was my nickname from when I was a kid.

"What's up, Tristan?" I asked, still holding the shirt close to my face. He leaned back on the couch before speaking.

"Look, we've been together four years now, and I don't think it's working anymore."

"Oh, yea? What made you come up with that?"

"Well, you know I've been bringing Bambi and a few others over here to try and spice up our sex life because you're a dead lay and not satisfying me the way I need."

"Are you fucking serious right now? You are breaking up with me for that fishy smelling pussy?"

"Calm down, Cady. I'm not breaking up with you; I just want Bambi to move in so she can teach you how to satisfy me daily, instead of once a week. You just lay there, and I don't even think you ever experienced an orgasm with me. I mean, come on; you should've at least done that by now."

I couldn't believe this nigga was basically making me a side chick for some bitch that clearly don't wash and having her move in.

"Nigga, HELL NO! There's no way in hell she's moving in with us." I shouted.

"Cady, you don't really have a say so."

"Oh, yes the fuck I do."

"You don't pay any fucking bills, you're not fucking me right, nor can you suck my dick good enough for me to cum. What is the use of you being here unless she comes and helps us out?" I was mad as hell, because he was not only my first, but he also had me doing shit I had no business doing.

"Fuck you, Tristan. I have been by your side all this time while you cheated on me over and over."

"Baby, I wasn't cheating. That was benefiting us in the long run."

"I'm going to let you believe that dumb shit. I allowed you to make me sit and watch how you fucked them or how you allowed them to suck your dick in hopes that I would learn. How about when you tried to get me to let the chic Erica eat my pussy. Yea, it wasn't happening no matter how much you begged."

"You didn't have to stay with me."

"I didn't, but I loved you, and I thought the feelings were mutual, but I was wrong. It's all good, though. I'm going back to my parents."

"Ok, I'll be here when you finish throwing your tantrum. Just know, nobody's going to want that nasty dried up pussy until you learn how to be a woman."

"You're saying I'm not a woman?"

"I'm saying, I'm the only man who will ever love you the way you need. I'm the only man that can have you saying my name."

"Goodbye asshole." I jumped in my car and called my mom. I was so hysterical by the time I got to the house she had to help me out the car.

"What's up, baby?" I was explaining to her what happened and couldn't help but see her checking the clock a few times.

"Ma, why do you keep looking at the clock?"

"Listen, go upstairs and get dressed. It's only ten, and your Uncle Donovan is having his 45th birthday tonight. I didn't invite you, because I didn't think you wanted to go, but fuck it. Let's turn that frown upside down. Fuck that nigga." I loved my mom. I was the only child, and she was my best friend.

"Can I invite Chanel?" She became my friend a few months after I moved here, because she was new as well. We clicked instantly, and became inseparable. The only reason I didn't call her first was because she was just getting off work at Rite Aid.

Of course she agreed, and we picked her up on the way. Fuck that stupid nigga. It was time for me to live my life. Shit, I was only 22, and I planned on acting like it.

Tristan

I don't know why Cady was saying she wasn't ok with me moving Bambi in. I pay all the motherfucking bills in here. That's the problem with these bitches nowadays, thinking because they live with you they can say what they want. Nah, fuck that. When you don't pay shit, you don't get to say shit.

I met Cady in high school, and even though I was her first at everything, she wasn't mine. I'll admit, I made it my business to bump into her that day in school. All the niggas were talking about the new chick and how bad she was. I took it as my cue to be the first to run up in that.

Yes, I was the captain of the football and basketball team and riding on a full scholarship anywhere I wanted. However, a truck hit me while I was sitting at a red light, and all chances of playing any sports were gone. I sued the shit out of the trucking company and walked away with a little over four million dollars.

Cady stayed by my side the entire time and never asked

for a dime. She is what any man would want in a woman, but she was naïve, dumb, and in my opinion; couldn't fuck. I tried everything to teach her, but nothing was working. It was as if she didn't get it. There was no way I could, or should spend my life with someone like that. It may sound fucked up, but I'm a man with needs.

I called Bambi up after she left and told her to come back over. She wasn't a dime piece, and there's really no need to describe her, because she's not that pretty. The reason why I stayed fucking her was because of her head game. That girl was vicious in the bedroom.

She decided to stay home, because she claimed to be tired after fucking. I went ahead and hit the club with some of my boys. They were already out, so I met up with them. When I got there, I noticed a party going on in the VIP area, which basically was one-half of the club.

"Yo' ain't that your girl walking up in here?" I saw Cady step inside with her friend Chanel. I was getting ready for her to come beg me to stay with her, when I noticed her roll her eyes and head to the party area.

I stared at them as the bouncer lifted the rope and let them through. I recognized the guy as her Uncle Donovan who is an old G that got out of jail for murder a few years ago.

"Let's go over there." Tony said, getting excited as he noticed the strippers were going in their direction. I picked my drink up and strolled over there with him.

Donovan came down to where we were, gave us a half hug and offered us to come up. One of the strippers came over to sit on my lap, and I could see Cady roll her eyes. I didn't care. Shit, she left. I enjoyed myself with a *'Cady who'* attitude.

<u>*Rory*</u>

I sat back observing everything and evrryone in the club, and watched my dad and his friend party up like they were 21. I'll admit, they seemed to be enjoying themselves; especially, when the strippers came out. The club was packed with women throwing themselves at any and every dude they thought were paid.

Miles and I watched two chicks walk in with, who appeared to be, one of their mom. Both of them were bad and hell; even mom had it going on. I found out later that it was Donovan's sister, his niece, and her best friend.

"Look at those two shorties." Miles said, smoking on the hookah.

"Yea, I peeped them, but they look mad young."

"Nigga, you only 26."

"I know right. But I don't want any dumb, young chick with no goals."

"Damn, man. I'm just trying to fuck one of them, and

you looking for wifey already." I lifted my cup and took a sip.

He and I stepped to the bathroom and were finishing up when we heard two people arguing outside the bathroom door. We glanced around, and it was one of the girls we just saw upstairs arguing with some dark-skinned dude. Shorty was bad, and I didn't understand why she was with this punk.

She had to be at least 5'5 with a brown cocoa-like complexion and light brown eyes. Her hair was cut in a bob; she had a dimple on one side of her face, and she a decent body. Her chest seemed to be maybe a C cup, and her ass was small but had a bounce to it.

She had on some blue strapless outfit with some silver heels. She didn't have on any make-up but you could see the lip-gloss shining. She had my attention, but I could see she was taken.

"We just broke up, and your ass in this club acting like a hoe already."

"Tristan, I just got here. You know that because you watched me walk in. And how am I being a ho? I'm just sitting there." I saw the tears running down her face, as he continued belittling and degrading her and she stood there and took it.

Miles and I walked past her, and she and I locked eyes for all of five seconds before he squeezed her cheeks and turned her face to him.

"Yo', this isn't any of my business but keep your hands off of her." I said.

"You're right, this is none of your business. Keep it moving, bro." I laughed and shook my head. I hated when niggas tried to test me.

"You good shorty?" I asked, and she nodded her head yes. I stepped in front of this corny ass nigga and lifted her chin. She wiped the tears from her eyes and smiled.

"Are you going to be ok if I leave you with him?" I couldn't lie; shorty was bad, and to see her going through that was pissing me off even more.

"Yes, I'm ok. Thank you." I kissed her cheek just to piss him off and kept walking.

"You fucking that nigga?" I heard him ask as we stepped off.

A few minutes later, she went to sit with the older

woman and her friend. I could tell she was telling them what happened, because they rolled their eyes in his direction. Shorty and I locked eyes again, and this time, I smiled and licked my lips. She grinned and pushed her hair on the side of her ear.

I saw dude walking in my direction, so I turned around to make sure he wasn't on any dumb shit.

"Listen my man; I don't appreciate you sticking your nose in my business like that." He tried to add bass in his voice.

"What kind of man talks to a woman like that or feels the need to put his hands on her?" I asked him and laughed.

"That's really none of your business, now is it?" I stepped in his face and noticed shorty walking my way with her friend.

"Nigga, you got five seconds to get the fuck out of here with that shit. I'm not her; I will fuck you up in here." He was about to say something when she stepped in between us. Her hands on my chest made my heart skip a beat. I didn't even know her, and she had me feeling some kind of way with just a touch.

"Please, Tristan. There's no need for this. We're not together anymore remember?"

"Oh, now we're not together, because you fucking him?"

"You know I'm not sleeping with him. I don't even know who this is."

"If you don't know who he is, then why he jump in our business?" She removed her hand from his chest but kept it on mines. Her friend kicked her foot, and she moved her hand.

"Nah, Ma. You can leave it there if you want. That's what a real man feels like." She turned around and smirked before pushing him away.

"A real man, huh? Well, real man or not, after you fuck her, you're going to feel less of a man." Shorty's eyes almost popped out of her head. I have no idea what he meant by it, but I knew since he was mad, he would elaborate.

"How dare you?" She stood there in total shock.

"Yea, you think this bitch a prize, but she can't fuck or suck dick. You're going to be mad as hell lying down with this dead lay." Tears just started flowing down her face, and I could tell she was embarrassed as hell.

"Yo', you a petty ass nigga. And if she can't fuck, it's probably because of the sorry ass nigga she laid down with." Her friend looked at me grinning while hugging her.

"Let's go, Cady." She snatched her arm away and went in the other direction. I saw my pops and her uncle walking over.

"What the hell is going on over here?" Donovan asked, as he started walking away, I explained to him what happened, and he had the nigga and his friend thrown out of the club altogether.

Not too long after, I saw her walking back with her friend. She didn't want to look in my direction, and I knew why.

"What kind of nigga says some fuck shit like that about his girl?" Miles asked me, as we stood outside smoking.

"I don't know, but she bad as hell. I would hate to think she couldn't fuck. Somebody who looks that good, has to throw down in the bedroom." I said still wondering why the nigga told her business.

"You stupid as hell. Man, I've fucked some of the baddest bitches, and she couldn't handle this dick and would tap out after only being in one position." He laughed.

"Right. Right. I ran up on a few like that too. I just don't see how she allowed him to talk to her like that. The nigga ain't shit." I said shaking my head.

"Nah, he's just hating, because he thinks she found something better. As you can see, they broke up, but they weren't broken up when he thought she was interested. For someone who said she couldn't fuck, he sure as hell didn't want her talking to anyone else." I had to agree.

We went back inside, and shorty was on the dance floor dancing. Her body was swaying with the music, and you could tell she was in a zone and in her own world. *Can't You See* by Total was playing.

In the middle of the day now baby

I seem to think of only you

Never thinking for a moment baby

I leaned back with my elbows on the bar watching her movement. She caught me staring and mouthed the words *thank you*. I just nodded my head and continued enjoying the show.

"She's pretty. Who is she?" My sister Angel asked sitting next to me. I could tell shorty was a little upset, because she rolled her eyes and turned around.

"Yea, she is, but she has some baggage I'm not trying to deal with. I'm trying to stay out of trouble, not get back in it."

"What kind of baggage?" I told her what happened, and she was just as mad the nigga said some foul shit like that. I grabbed my sisters' hand and stepped on the dance floor with her. The DJ had *Touch Me, Tease Me* by Case playing.

My uncle had the music from the 90's and early 2000's playing and everybody was out of the dance floor. Miles was dancing with the girls' friend, and my sister and I stayed out there a bit longer.

"I just wanted to say thank you again for earlier. I apologize for him stepping to you." She spoke in my ear from behind, as I sat on the barstool. I turned around to speak to her, when dude must've got back in somehow.

"I leave, and you in his face." He was squeezing her arm and yelling. I hit dude so hard he hit the floor and was out cold.

I had about enough of him, and it was time to show this nigga what's up. I know I had no idea who she was; but I didn't tolerate a man abusing a woman.

"I know I shouldn't say this, but thank you for doing that." She stood in front of me licking her lips, and I couldn't resist. I leaned down and kissed her; tasting her lip-gloss. She backed up a little and smiled before her friend rushed her off. It was the last time I saw her, and it's probably for the best after knocking her man out. I finished the rest of my drink, grabbed my sister and Miles, and left.

Cadence

"Chanel that man was fine as hell; who was he?" I askd my friend about the guy from the club last night as if she knew.

"Girl, I don't know. I met him the same time as you." Chanel and I were on our way to retro fitness to work out.

When we got inside, we took the tank off, left oir sports bra on, stepped on the elliptical and put our earphones in our ear. A few minutes later, I felt someone tap my shoulder. I turned around and looked into the eyes of the man who knocked Tristan's dumb ass out. I stopped the machine and snatched the earphones out to hear what he had to say.

"Hi." I smiled, as he helped me down off the machine.

"So, we meet again, huh? And this time, I don't see that fuck nigga with you." I couldn't help but laugh.

"No, he's not here. I'm here with my best friend, Chanel." She was oblivious to it all.

He stared me up and down; which made me feel a little uncomfortable. When he licked those lips, I felt a weird feeling in between my legs I never felt with Tristan. If I didn't know

any better, I would say some of my insides were leaking out.

This man was tall and brown-skinned, with hazel eyes.

He had tattoos up and down his arms, on his hands, legs, and

you can tell on his chest. The tank top didn't leave much to the

imagination. His muscles weren't too big but just right, and his

imprint looked like it would kill me.

What the hell was I doing lusting over a man that could

probably break me in two with what it looked like in between

his legs? He folded his arms across his chest and stared at me.

"Are you done?"

"Huh?" I asked looking back up at him.

"Are you done?" I looked at him confused.

"Do you like what you see? I mean, you've only been

staring since I pulled you away from the machine." I put my

head down, and he could tell I was embarrassed.

"I do, but..." He cut me off.

"But what?"

"But I shouldn't be looking at you like that."

"Why not?"

"I'm sure your girlfriend would get mad." Just as I said it, the girl he was dancing with popped up.

"Hi, I'm Angel. What's your name?" She extended her hand for me to shake.

"Hi. I'm Cadence. But everyone calls me Cady for short."

"Cadence, huh? That's sexy as hell. Can I call you that instead?" Hos voice was smooth and rogigh at the same time.

"Yea, I guess."

"Anyway, he's being rude. I'm his sister." W eshook hands.

"Aren't you the one I saw last night kissing him?" I covered my mouth and went back by Chanel, who was now talking to his friend.

"Girl, let's go." I saw her looking at me like I was crazy.

"Ok, Miles it was nice meeting you."

"Can I call you later?" He asked her, as we went into the locker room. She nodded her head yes and followed behind me.

I told her what happened, and she thought the shit was

funny, but I didn't. I looked around and there was only one shower available, so I let her go first.

I stepped in after and let the hot water beat down on me. I wrapped the towel around me when I was finished and walked to the mirror to wipe it down, because the steam covered it. I gasped, when I noticed dude standing behind me leaning on the wall. I turned around so quick, the towel fell to the floor.

I couldn't pick it up because my feet were stuck. He bent down, picked it up, and wrapped it around me. The way his hands felt on my body gave me a euphoric feeling.

"What are you doing in here?" He stood in front of me, and before I knew it, his tongue was in my mouth.

The way our tongues found a rhythm instantly made me think this was right. The feeling and moisture brewing between my legs had my body shaking. I placed my hand on his head, and he pulled my body closer. This felt so right; yet it was wrong. I didn't know this man, but my body was reacting to him as if we belonged together.

"We have to stop. This is not right."

"What's not right?" He asked and trailed kisses down my neck.

"We don't know each other." He put me up on the sink and lifted one of my legs. I didn't know what was happening with us, and I've never been with another man; however, I was just letting it happen.

"Are you ok, Cadence?" I tried to answer him, but there was no way I could. He took his finger and rubbed it up and down my pussy.

"Yes. Oh, yes." I moaned in his ear.

"You like how this feels?" He continued to rub his fingers, and when he touched what felt like a ball on my pussy, I screamed out.

He covered my mouth with his. It felt like my insides were coming out on his fingers. There was so much leaking out, I jumped back. He grinned and put his head down there. My legs were on top of his shoulder, while he was on his knees, face first in my pussy. The feeling came back, and before I knew it, I was leaking on his face again.

"You good baby?" My breathing was erratic, and it

took me a few minutes to calm down. He stood in front of me, and his dick was trying to break free. I looked down nervous as hell.

"Don't worry. I know you're not ready for him yet." He helped me off the sink and had to catch me, as I almost fell.

My entire body was weak, and I can't ever remember feeling like this when my ex ate me out. This man had me open, and I just met him last night. The embarrassment washed over me, and I knew he was able to tell. I stepped back in the shower and closed the curtain. When I came out, he was gone.

"Girl, what the hell was going on in here?" I heard Chanel saying as she came in. I shut the water off when I was done and went to get dressed. I didn't know if I should tell her or keep my secret.

"Nothing, why?" She looked me up and down and burst out laughing.

"Bitch, that nigga made everybody get out, and then, locked the door." I told her what happened, and she almost lost it.

"About damn time somebody made you have an

orgasm. That shit was beautiful, wasn't it?" I told her yes, and we finished getting dressed. Women began coming in and out, but no one mentioned anything about the doors being locked.

We stepped out, and both guys and his sister were gone. I looked around the entire gym, and he was nowhere in sight. I can't believe I let this man give me my first experience with an orgasm, and he just up and left.

"Don't worry about it girl. Look at it like this. Now, you know what that feeling is, so don't expect anything less from a man that goes down on you. If he can't bring you the same feeling, there's no need to be with him."

"Let's go, girl. I'm tired as hell after that."

"Yup, that was definitely an orgasm he gave you. Shit, will put a bitch straight to sleep afterwards." I laughed at her, because she wasn't a virgin and had her first one not too long ago either.

I don't think people understand that an orgasm doesn't just happen each time you have sex. Lord knows it never did with me.

Chanel dropped me off at home, I walked in, and went

straight to my room to lie down.

"I put yo ass to sleep, huh?" I jumped up off the bed and saw this man strolling in my room.

"How in the hell did you get in here? Better yet, how did you know where I lived?" Just as I asked, my uncle came in.

"Hey. How's my favorite niece?"

"I'm your only niece. I'm good. What are you doing here?" He hugged me and introduced me to his friends' son Rory.

"Hi, Rory. It's nice to see you again."

"Oh, you two met before." He pushed me back to wait for my answer.

"Remember he was at the party last night."

"Yea, and I saw her at the gym not too long ago." He said, licking his lips, as he looked down on his phone. This man was driving me crazy, and he knew it.

"Well, anyway. His pops just transferred all his businesses into his name and one of them happen to be Retro Fitness." I shook my head laughing thinking that's how he was able to lock shit down.

"That's good. Well, it's nice to meet you again. If you'll excuse me, I was about to take a nap." My uncle kissed my forehead and told me he would see me later. I stood there with my arms folded waiting for him to leave.

"Oh, you want me to go, too?" He asked, placing his phone in his pocket.

"Yea." He came closer, and I found myself becoming intimidated. I sat down on my bed, and he took a seat next to me.

"Why do you fall back when I get close to you?" He turned my face to him.

"I don't know. It's a habit I guess."

"Damn, that nigga been breaking you down. How long have you been with him?"

"Four years." I felt a few tears drop and he used his thumbs to wipe them away.

"Baby girl, from here on out, don't allow him or any man to make you feel less of a woman. Your beauty threatens a man like that, and what he knows you have. He probably thinks, if he beats you down enough, you'll stay with him."

"Well, it's been working. He's the only man I've ever been with." I truthfully replied.

"Hmph." He said and stood up. He got down on one knee and put his lips to mines again.

"I have to go, but I wanna finish this conversation another day. Try not to let him get to you." He haded towards the door and turned around.

"Oh, your pussy taste really good in my mouth." He winked and walked out the door.

I knew he was lying, because Tristan always told me it didn't have a taste. That motherfucker just pissed me off. Fuck him. I told myself I wasn't fucking with him anymore. I already had one man that broke me down; there was no way I was about to have two. I laid on my bed and fell asleep.

Miles

The night of my uncles' friend, Donovan's, birthday party, Rory and I made plans to move to Texas. Fortunately, his dad made the decision to turn all his businesses over to him and I. Rory's dad always looked at me like his son and offered me some of his businesses. I don't know why, but I didn't turn him down.

Even though we were now owners of a few gyms, and a couple of restaurants, it still didn't seem like enough. Don't get me wrong, cash wise it was more than enough, but when you didn't have anyone to share it with, what's the purpose?

Oh, I'm Miles; Rory's cousin, brother, or whatever else we call ourselves. We're not related by blood, but who needs that to be family nowadays. Shit, blood relatives fuck you over quicker than a stranger.

Rory and I have been friends since kindergarten. We both grew up in two parent households and our parents didn't even know each other. Throughout the years, they've met up on a few occasions from us getting in trouble.

You see, our parents all worked 9-5 jobs, showed up at any sporting events we were in, and even went to parent-teacher conferences. We didn't sell drugs, nor did we need to.

Our parents had both of us enrolled in boxing classes that we had to attend Monday through Friday for two hours a day unless we had basketball. They made sure we stayed off the streets. If I wasn't at his house, it was vice versa.

Rory and I still stayed in trouble and many of times, we would be outside in the courts playing basketball, and street dudes would test us. Of course, because we weren't good enough, or so they thought. Its crazy because we caught our first charge at seventeen, which is when we broke our parents' hearts.

Rory and I were walking down the street coming from boxing practice, when a few of the street dudes walked behind us talking shit. We ignored them for as long as we could.

"Look at these punk ass niggas." One of them said. Rory had his earphones on, but once I saw them behind us, I took one of mine off.

"What motherfucker?" I yelled back at him. Rory turned around and dropped his bag on the ground. He was never really one who liked to talk.

We realized they were just talking, so we kept it moving. I walked in the store with Rory, and when we stepped out, the two of them were waiting with guns in our face.

"Get that shit out my face." Rory said, taking his stuff off.

"Nah, you think you're tough, because y'all niggas box. Let me see you box your way out of this." The other one said.

I looked at him, and vice versa, and before they knew what hit them, we were beating the brakes off of they ass. There was so much blood, we thought we killed them. A crowd had gathered, and no one was able to stop us until the cops came.

We went to Middlesex County Jail, and they were going to try us as adults because of the beating. They had us stay in there for two days before we got a bail hearing. The judge said we used our hands for weapons, and even though people fight all the time, we were boxers, so our hands were deadly. Our lawyer got us out on bail but that didn't help.

The dudes we beat up were in a gang, so their enemy approached us asking Rory and I, to join them. We refused over and over but they were persistent.

Anyway, after months of asking, we finally gave in and became members of the "Bloods" gang. We didn't need any initiation, because they knew what we were working with.

In the end, the lawyer got us off, because the video outside the store showed them pulling guns out on us. The judge said, we were protecting ourselves and couldn't see it any other way once he saw the video.

Unfortunately, once we joined the gang, trouble constantly found us. Both of us ended up doing three years for getting caught with a concealed weapon. Luckily, they put us in the same jail because of overcrowding. We met tons of people inside and made more brothers for life.

Now both of us are looking to get out the gang, but you know, once you're in, that's it. That's where Donovan comes in for us. Not only did he just get out of jail and the drug game a few years ago, he was still the one in charge of any and all

"Bloods" on the East Coast.

He couldn't promise us a way out, but he did sit down and have meetings on our behalf like he did when anyone wanted to leave the gang life. He told us we were *"Bloods"* for life.

Fortunately, there were so many kids trying to be in a gang, we weren't needed. The only thing we had to do was be ready if there was ever a war. That was good enough for us and our lives have been fine ever since.

Now, I'm sitting here picking up this new chick Chanel, I met the other night. She was light-skinned with shoulder length hair, had light brown eyes, a bit of freckles, and some thick lips. Her body was average, but the way she wore her clothes had you thinking otherwise. She had thick thighs, and her hips were just the right size. I loved my woman with meat on her bones.

She came out wearing tight black pants with some riding boots, a sweater that came down in the front showing off some of her cleavge, and her hair was in a ponytail.

"Hey, I'm sorry I had you waiting."

"That's ok. It was well worth it." She smiled and put her seatbelt on.

We went to some restaurant in Belmar and walked the beach not too long after. I found out she worked at Rite Aid and was taking a few classes online. She really wanted to do the campus life, but she had hectic work hours. She lived alone and is currently single due to catching her man cheating.

"What about you?" She asked catching me off guard.

"What do you mean?"

"I'm telling you my whole life story. Tell me something about yourself." I told her how Rory and I met and left out any gang affiliation.

You either have chicks who love being with a gang member or the one's that hauled ass. I was feeling shortly; if she stays around long enough, then I'll tell her. For now, I felt there was no need.

I parked in front of her house and turned my car off.

"You want to come in?" It was only ten-thirty. *I told Rory I would meet him at twelve, so why not?* I thought to myself.

She had a one-bedroom apartment that had a small lake behind it. She had a black living room set with a 60-inch TV inside. Her kitchen was small, but it had a table set inside. She showed me her bathroom, which was very clean and trust me; a nigga noticed it.

Now, her bedroom was a different story. She had a black king-sized bedroom set. The entire room was black and red too. The shades were black, and her curtains were red. She had a flat screen hanging on the wall and a plush carpet. Her dresser had all female products on it, and I couldn't help notice the sheer red canopy draped over her bed.

"Damn, girl. What are you trying to do to a nigga in here?"

"If you stay around long enough, maybe you'll see." She pecked my lips and went back in the living room. She offered me water and sat with me on the love seat.

"How can you afford this on a Rite Aid salary?" She started laughing.

"My dad died and left me some money. I could've moved into a bigger place, but I like being this tight. Plus, the money he left me won't last a lifetime, so there was no need to live above my means. I just upgraded a little."

"I can respect that." We kicked it for a bit longer, and I have to say I enjoyed every minute with her. Shorty was mad cool and down to earth. I got up to leave and pulled her close to me.

"I don't know about you, but I want to see you again." I told her and olaced a soft kiss on her neck.

"I guess I can find a spot one day this week to fit you in."

"Oh, yea? Let me see if this will help convince you." I cupped her face and slip my tongue in her mouth still tasting the mint we had at the restaurant on it. She wrapped her hands around my neck, and I could feel myself becoming aroused and backed up. Since I was feeling her, I decided to see where we would take it. She looked down and laughed. I opened the door and pecked her lips once more before I left.

I ended up at the bar with Rory and thought about her the entire time. I wanted to go back over there, but she sent a message two hours ago saying she was on her way to bed. I went to my ex's house and let her release all my stress.

<u>Chanel</u>

45

What's up, y'all? I'm Chanel; Cady's best friend. I met her when we were both juniors who moved from different states. I got here before her, so I knew what it was like to feel alone.

Anyway, the closer we got, the more I hated Tristan. I saw the way he treated her on a daily basis, and it bothered me that she wouldn't leave.

He never hit her, or so she says, but in the last four years, the emotional and mental scars he put on her was guaranteed to keep her fucked up forever. That's why, when dude stepped up at the club, I was praying they hit it off so she could get away from Tristan. The nigga ain't shit. I remembered when he tried to fuck me while she was in class one day.

He came to my house and I had just got off. He claimed he was waiting for Cady to get out of school, and she was meeting him there. I was in the kitchen when he came up *kissing my neck. I turned around, and hit that nigga so hard in his stomach he doubled over. I don't play that shit.*

"What the fuck, Chanel?" He leaned over holding his stomach. I had a mixing spoon in my hand, so when he tried it, I jabbed him with it.

"Don't ever think that's ok. It's never going to happen, and just because I'm a female, don't think I won't hit your ass again with something bigger." I knew I couldn't beat him, but I used all my strength, and it worked. His ass grabbed the keys and left.

I told Cady what happened, and of course, he lied and said I wanted him. She stopped talking to me for like a month until, of course, he brought another chick over to try and teach her how to fuck.

I didn't understand why she stayed with him. I mean, he gave her gonorrhea twice, and she had a few yeast infections, but I guess my mom was right when she said, *'a woman would know when she's had enough'*. She will break free when she's ready.

I was just mad it's been four years, and she still hasn't

really left him. She goes home all the time, and ends up right back over there. Not the kid; I wish a nigga would.

Miles seems to be a nice guy, but only time will tell. He wasn't super fine, and I was cool with that. I didn't want a gorgeous man who would worry more about his looks and women, than settling down with one chick.

Miles was dark-skinned, which I loved. He had a goatee, with the sideburns to match. He was covered with tattoos all over, and his body looked like it was carved out specifically for him. And his eyes were a light grayish color that looked weird; kind of like a cat.

He and I hit it off well, and I saw myself falling for him. Unfortunately, I know his ex Tory, and I can't stand her trifling ass. I caught her out with my ex Mike and beat her ass. I knew if I decided to be with Miles, she was going to be a problem.

****

I was bending over taking stuff out of boxes when I felt

someone come up behind me. I jumped up and turned around to see Miles.

"Hey sexy."

"Boy, don't be pressing up on me like that." I punched his arm.

"What time you get off? I want to take you out to eat."

"I get off at five and what makes you think I want to go out with you?" He leaned in, slipped his tongue in my mouth and I swear, I came on myself. We heard someone clearing their throat and looked up to see his ex, Tory.

"Wow Miles. I see you're slumming for your next victim." I threw my price check gun on the floor and stepped to her, but he moved me to the side.

"Go 'head with that shit, Tory."

"I'm going. Oh, thanks for the sex last night. I slept like a baby." He shook his head.

"I can see you're still petty. Miles, go handle your business." I waved him off and picked my stuff up.

"Can I still take you out later?" I shook my head no. I wasn't playing these games with him. I knew he would continue fucking her, and I've had enough drama with her.

"I know you're not begging Miles. That's not even your style. Especially, not someone who isn't up to par with what you're used to." She said, looping her arm in his. I pinched the bridge of my nose to stay calm.

"Miles, I know I'm not some stuck up materialistic bitch you're accustomed to, and since it seems like she knows your type, this isn't going to work. I enjoyed your company, but this is my job, where I make my living. Can you and her please leave? As she said, I can't afford to get fired; I don't have no one taking care of me."

He snatched his arm away from her and left with her running behind him. Whew! I'm glad the shit ended before it got started.

I get off work at five, and since it was Friday, Cady and I decided to go out and party. She and I had a great time too.

When I got home, I saw flowers and a note by my door. I left the flowers and picked up the note.

Chanel

I hope you're not going to let her interfere with what we both know is going to happen. Yea, I slept with her, I won't deny that, but you and I just met. Can you really say you're bothered? Look, call me.

I crumbled the paper up and tossed it in the trash, hopped in the shower and took my ass to bed. I had the next two days off, and a bitch was happy.

I had a few missed calls from Miles and a text from Cady. I threw the phone on my bed and cleaned my house. I stayed home all weekend and caught up on much-needed rest.

<u>Cadence</u>

Rory and I have been texting one another sporadically over the last month. I wasn't ready for a relationship, and neither was he. We were supposed to meet up a few times, but one of us always canceled.

Tonight, he asked me to stop by his house to pick some stuff up for my uncle. I threw on some sweats and a T-shirt with some Uggs. I wasn't trying to impress him anymore. It seemed like we were better off as friends.

He was on the phone, when he answered the door, so I followed behind him and waited. He came back in with two boxes. After he placed them in my car, he invited me back in for a drink.

"Damn, this is the first time I can actually embrace how beautiful you are." He said, leaning over the counter. I put my head down blushing.

"Thank you."

"Lift your head up." He got up from his chair, stood in

front of me, lifted my shirt over my head and took my boots and pants off and managed to keep his eyes on me the entire time. I don't know why I allowed him to do it.

"Damn shorty, you bad as hell." I felt so uncomfortable. Before I could say anything, he picked me up and carried me in his bedroom.

"Can I make love to you?"

"Rory, I've only been with one other person. I don't think I can satisfy you." He licked his lips and took his shirt off.

"Don't worry about it. I'm going to show you how to please me. First, let me taste you again."

"Are you sure?" His mouth covered mines while his fingers ran up and down my treasure box.

He moved down to my chest, pushed both of them together and flicked back and forth. The way he sucked, had my pussy soaking wet. When he found his spot, he latched on like a baby sucking on a nipple.

I'm not big on men placing their fingers inside me, but he was so gentle and found a spot inside that drove me crazy. I felt my bottom half grinding on them as he continued sucking.

The feeling I had in the gym bathroom was coming back, and this time, it felt stronger than before.

"Ahhhh, yesssss…." I yelled out and grabbed his head. My pussy felt like a wave was flowing through, and it had a beat to it. I couldn't explain what he was taking my body through, but I knew I wanted more.

"You like that Cadence?" I was trying to control my breathing.

"Yes. Oh, God yes." I was having an outer body experience, as he made me have another one. This time, my legs started shaking and my body jerked.

"Are you ready for me?" I nodded my head yes, even though I knew I wasn't. He came out of all his clothes, and his body was magnificent. There was no other way to explain it. He climbed on top of me, placing the head inside slowly.

"Oh, shit." I cried out.

"You ok?" I kept shaking my head yes knowing I wasn't. I just wanted the initial part of entering me to be over. He stuck more inside, and I thought I was going to die.

"Relax, baby. It's going to hurt at the beginning. Don't

think about the pain. It makes it a little easier." Shit, that was easy for him to say. I wasn't ripping his shit open.

He kissed my lips and continued pushing through. The way he kissed made my body relax, and I was overflowing down there. When he got in, he took slow strokes to get me used to it.

"How does it feel now?"

"It still hurts a little, but keep going. I don't want you to stop." Tristan had a decent size, but it was nowhere like his. Rory kept my pussy wet, while Tristan would fuck me dry. The pain subsided with every stroke, and my body began to relax.

"Shit, this feels good Rory." He smiled and kept going.

"I want you to try it out on top." He told me and pulled out to roll over on his back.

"Get on your knees first, and take your time going down. If you go too fast, you may hurt yourself." I did what he told me, and it felt like he was touching my stomach, but I wanted to please him, so I stayed up there.

"Now, move in circular motions." I did what he said and heard a soft moan leave his lips.

"Shit, this feels good." I said out loud, but not meaning to. He grinned and kept instructing me.

"Put your hands on my chest and lift up and down on it." I looked, and my juices came down, as I watched it go in and out. I don't know what came over me, but I went faster and faster.

"Yea, Cadence, just like that. Fuck, it feels real good." He had his hands on my hips pumping inside. After a few minutes, he had me stand on my feet, as he held my hands. I went up and down, slow, and then fast; and he went crazy.

"Baby, look how sexy that shit looks. Damn, keep riding me like that." I went faster, and he squeezed my hands tighter and released himself in the condom.

"Fuck, that was good for someone who claims she didn't know what to do. Come here." He pulled me on top of him and kissed me aggressively.

I rolled off to get up, but he grabbed me by the waist and had me turn over. He showed me how to throw it back when he was hitting it from behind, and finished making love to me all night. It was the best sexual experience I ever had in my life.

******************************.

The last couple of weeks, I was at his house almost every day learning new things. I even had him teach me how to please him orally. It took me a little longer for that, but once I mastered it, he would tap out.

"Baby, you a pro now." I smacked his arm, as I laid on his chest after one of our love-making sessions.

"Rory, what are we doing? I mean, what is this?" He kissed my forehead and told me to go to sleep. He and I still had conflicting schedules, but if either one of us wanted to have sex, we made time for it. I had become addicted to sexing him.

The next day, I was bored, so I called Chanel to see what she was doing. I didn't feel like sititng it in the house.

"Bitch, let's go to the gym. We haven't been in a while." I said.

"I guess, since Rory's been working you out, there's no

need for you to go." She joked.

"Whatever, Chanel." I grabbed my bag and drove with her over to Retro. I saw Rory's car there, but didn't bother stopping by his office. I figured he was busy, and I would see him later.

We were walking past this office, and I swore I heard moaning, and the closer we got, the louder it got.

"Don't do it, Cady. You may walk into something that you don't want to see." Chanel tried to grab my arm.

I had to see what was going on; but I was praying the door was locked. When it wasn't, I pushed it open slowly and gasped. Some woman was sitting on his lap naked, straddling him in the chair. His hands were roaming on her back as she went up and down on him.

"Oh Rory, this feels so good." I felt the tears falling, and that's when he noticed me standing there. He locked eyes with me, and I closed the door just as quietly as I went in.

"Let's go, Chanel." I looped my arms in hers and wiped my eyes.

"What happened?" She was looking at me crazy, as I

rushed her to the car. I saw him running out, and she didn't unlock the doors fast enough. He turned me around, and I saw the bite mark on his shoulder as he put his shirt on.

"What's up, Cadence? You're just going to leave?"

"Oh, did you expect me to stay to finish watching the show? I mean, I could get some popcorn if you want."

"I'm not saying that, and you know it. I know you heard me calling you."

"It's ok, Rory. I'm not mad."

"What you mean, you're not mad? You're fucking crying." I wiped my eyes and the snot and looked up at him.

"Is that better? No more crying. You feel better?" I gave him a fake smile.

"Why are you upset? We're not together."

"You know what, you're right. How stupid of me to catch feelings for you? How stupid of me to believe you were any different than him?"

"Listen, don't ever compare me to him. I'm not going to lie and say I didn't enjoy every minute with you because I did and always do, but I'm not ready to settle down right now.

I'm not the nigga you want to love."

"How do you know what I want? Did you ever ask me?"

"I'm the one to blame in all this, so I'm sorry if you're hurt." He tried to hug me and I pushed him off.

"Don't worry about it, Rory. I'll be ok. Just continue to do you."

"That's how it's going to be?"

"Yea. We can still be friends. That's what you want right?" I asked him putting my bag in the car. Chanel was already inside looking on her phone.

"Let me come by later so we can talk about this." I scoffed up a laugh and felt the tears flowing again. He tried to wipe them, and I smacked his hands away.

"No thanks." O scoffed up a laugh.

"You know, Rory? All you had to do was tell me. I know it was a surprise I walked in, but you still knew there were other women in your life. I didn't expect for you to fall in love with me, but I did think you respected me more. I guess, I'll see you around." I kissed his cheek and shut the door.

Chanel pulled off, and I saw him with his hands over the top of his head watching us.

The next few weeks were pure torture for me. He called me non-stop, and if he came by, I had my parents tell him I wasn't there. I felt like my heart was bleeding, and there was nothing I could do to stop it. I felt like a fool for falling in love with a man that didn't feel the same.

I wa so mad that one day, Tristan called me over, and I went by to see him. One thing led to another, and even though he wasn't Rory, I still wanted sex. I made him wear a condom both times I slept with him.

At first, he was having a fit, but I told him it was the only way. I made sure I picked them up before I went to his house so there was no excuse for not using them. I would never let him run up in me raw again.

I sexed him so good, he was calling out my name. I smiled when this nigga told me he couldn't cum anymore. Rory taught me well.

<u>*Rory*</u>

5 Months Later…

I was missing the hell out of Cadence, but I couldn't give her what she wanted; which was all of me. When pops turned the businesses over to me, I dove head first to make sure we stayed making money. And you know with more money, comes more problems and more bitches.

That day Cadence walked in my office at the gym and saw me fucking some chick, I knew I broke her heart. Deep down, I could tell she had feelings for me. The hurt in her eyes tore me up, as she wiped them and kept saying she was ok. I tried to reach out to her, but she wasn't trying to hear it.

It's been a few months since I spoke to her, but I made up my mind to call her anyway. I couldn't even get mad at what I heard, because it was my fault for hurting her.

"Damn, Cady. That's twice you had me tapping out first. That pussy is better and lethal." Whoever the guy in the

background was, said.

"Whatever. I've only slept with you twice."

"Yea, but both times you had me saying your name and tapping out." I was mad, but I smiled when I heard him say it. It means she was throwing it on niggas now.

"Where you learn that shit from? Who taught you how to fuck like?"

"Wouldn't you like to know?" I could hear the sarcasm in her voice.

"Don't get cute bitch. Just because you learned how to fuck don't mean shit. You're still that broke down bitch."

"Alright, it's time for me to go."

"No, I'm sorry. Don't go. I can't see myself without you."

"You just don't want anyone to get this. You don't want me." I had heard enough. I hit disconnect on the phone and threw my phone across the room.

Not only was I mad he was degrading her again, but he only wanted her because of what I taught her.

"Yo, what's up? Why you mad?" Miles walked in and

sat in the chair across from me.

"Nothing man. I'm good."

"Nigga, I know you. You're not tearing shit up for nothing. What's up?"

"Man, chick got me going through it right now." He looked at me strangely, because he knew I didn't have a woman.

"Who you talking about? You're not serious with anyone." I ran my hand down my face before I spoke.

"Cadence."

"Cadence. What the hell? I didn't know you two were messing around." I explained to him what occurred between us and what I just heard on the phone.

"Let me get this right." He leaned over and had hos elbows on his knees.

"You taught her how to fuck, then she turned around and threw it on your ass, only for you to get caught with your pants down literally; and now, she back with her ex. He wants her back, because of what you showed her?" I nodded my head yes, and he fell out the chair laughing.

"What's so funny?"

"Man, I think she has you stuck, because you're feeling her more than you want to." I didn't want to look at it that way, but he was probably right. He and I spoke a little longer and he went on hos way.

✳✳✳✳✳✳✳✳✳✳✳✳✳✳✳✳✳✳✳✳✳✳✳✳✳✳✳✳

I was in my office at the gym a few days later, when I heard my sister asking someone were they attending her party. I stuck my head out and saw it was Cadence and Chanel. I sat my ass back down to finish doing some paperwork and to let my mind wander to those nights we made love to each other.

The night of my sister's party, Cadence looked beyond sexy. I found myself staring at her most of the night.

"Go talk to her." Angel said sitting next to me.

"Nah, she's having fun. I don't want to bother her." I took a sip of my drink. My sister grabbed my hand and dragged me to Cadence.

"Cadence my brother misses you, and I know you miss

64

him, now y'all need to make up." She walked away and Cadence snatched my hand and led me down some back hall.

"What do you want from me Rory?"

"Nothing. I just wanted to see if you were ok." She stared into my eyes and kissed me.

"What are you doing girl?" She trailed kisses down my neck and stuck her hand in my jeans. I moved her hand and took her in the bathroom.

"I want you, Rory." She said in between kisses.

"I want you too, baby." I locked the bathroom door and slid her down on my dick.

"Fuck girl. I missed this."

"I missed you, too. Why does it feel so good?" I was pumping harder inside her. Her screams were driving me insane.

"Rory, I'm about to cum. Oh shit, baby. Here I cummmmmm...." I exploded inside her with no regrets. I know damn well we knew better. I sat her on the sink and wet some paper towels to clean her up.

"Did you use a condom when you fucked him?" She

put her head down like she was ashamed.

"Yea. How did you know?"

"I called your phone, and you must of hit answer instead of ignore."

"Oh, my God. Did you hear us?" I removed her hands from her face.

"No. I just heard the way he spoke to you, I guess when you were finished. Why do you let him speak to you like that?"

"I don't know. I guess, I'm just used to it now." I could tell she was upset, so I dropped it for now.

"So you threw it on him?" She smiled and stuck her tongue out.

"Just know, that's the last time I want him touching you." She looked up at me and grinned.

"Oh, yea. You're not my man." I went to speak, but there was a knock on the door. We stepped out the bathroom holding hands.

"It's about time." Miles said, when we walked back upstairs and enjoyed the rest of the party together.

Candace came home with me after and the minute I

unlocked the door, we were all over each other. I bent her over the side of the couch and spread her open from behind. I went back and forth licking and sucking on her clit and ass.

"Oh, my God, Oh my God, oh shhhhiiit." Her orgasm was so strong, I could feel her clit pulsating in my mouth.

She pushed me back and sucked my man back to life. The way she cupped my balls and jerked my dick had me ready to nut. She put a little spit on it, then gave me the best sloppy wet head ever.

"Damn, just like that." I guided her head up and down. When she felt me cumming, she went faster and faster, causing me to squirt all my babies down her throat. I had taught her so much, and it felt like she got better and better each time.

She straddled my man and kissed me. When she slid down; it was like I was in heaven all over again. She put her hands in mine and rode me on her feet. Popping up and down just the way I like it.

"You like this baby?" She asked in between moaning.

"Hell, yea. I love it. Don't stop." She went faster, and I felt her clit getting harder.

"I'm about to cum, Rory. Are you cumming with me?"

"If you want me to."

"Yes, I do. Cum with me baby." I covered her mouth with mines and fucked her harder.

"Fuck, Cadence. This pussy is going to have me killing niggas. Shit girl, what are you doing to me?"

"What are you doing to me Rory? I've missed you so much." She said, riding faster.

"I'm in love with you, Cadence."

"I'm in love with you too, Rory."

"Awww shit, baby. Here I cum."

"Me too, Daddy. Oh, God. Yes, yes, yessss......" We both laid there panting and trying to catch our breath. I pulled her on top of me. Neither one of us spoke a word as we listened to one another breathe. I pushed the hair out her face and kissed her forehead.

"I meant what I said Cadence. I'm in love with you." She lifted her head and pecked my lips.

"I'm in love with you too, Rory. I just don't want to get hurt. Where do we go from here?" She asked, as if I was supposed to know.

"I don't know. We both just admitted to being in love, so I guess the next step would be to make us official." I didn't say a word. I wasn't sure if I was ready for a commitment. Could I remain faithful? Would I hurt her? I had so many thoughts going through my mind. I know I didn't want to ever see her hurting like that over me again.

"Cadence, I don't know what this is we have. All I know is, when you weren't in my life, I couldn't focus. I missed everything about you. I want to give you all of me, but I don't want to hurt you either. I don't ever want to break your heart or bring that pain to you again."

"I don't want you to hurt me either, so if you're not ready, I can respect it. All I ask is, you keep it honest with me. You don't want a relationship right now, ok, I get that, but I can't sit around waiting or watching you give yourself to other women." I heard her sniffling, and I felt fucked up again.

"Don't cry baby. I didn't say I was going to be with anyone else. I want to be with you, but I have to clear up some loose ends. I want to be with you without any distractions or anything from my past."

"So what are you saying?" She sat up wiping her eyes.

"I'm saying don't give up on me."

"I would never give up on you."

"I am going to give you the world Cadence, because you deserve it."

"I don't want the world. All I want is you." She sucked on my bottom lip and rubbed her hand up and down my shaft until he woke up. We made love all through the night.

The next day, I had to give her a ride home, because she drove to the party with Chanel and I tbrought her home. As we were walking out the door, my ex, Taylor came strolling up.

"So is she the one you left me for?" Cadence asked me for the keys and went to the car.

"Taylor, I haven't talked to you in over two months. Why you here?" I could see Cadence in the car looking down on her phone.

"I miss us. I miss this." She kissed on my ear and put her hand on my crotch. I removed it and twisted her arm back.

"What are you doing, Rory?" Taylor cried out.

"Taylor, if you just came over here and asked me if she was the reason I don't fuck with you anymore, why would you put your hands on her dick? You on some straight disrespectful shit."

"So, you're bending my arm back for her? Is she your girl?"

"Yup, and I don't ever wanna see or hear about you disrespecting her in any way. She has done nothing to you. She even gave you the respect to converse with me alone, when she could've stayed right here."

"Damn, what did she do to you? I've never seen you act like this before; not even over me." She started wiping the tears that were falling.

Taylor and I used to date for a few years until she slept with one of my boys when I was in jail. You know how that goes.

"That's your girl, but isn't she the one who caught us in your office fucking? You disrespected her first; yet, I'm the bad one." I thought about what she said before I responded.

"You're right, and she left me alone. We weren't

together at the time, but you can bet it won't happen again.

Now, if you'll excuse me, I have to go." I heade to my cqr.

"Oh, don't come back over here and lose my number."

I sat in the car and kissed Cadence. I saw Taylor walk off

pissed, and I didn't care. I had the woman I wanted.

Tristan

This bitch must be crazy if she thinks I'm letting her go. Yea, I fucked up and did her dirty, but I never thought she would leave me. The night I told her Bambi was staying here, I knew she was done. I guess, after so many years of me shitting on her, she had had enough.

I almost flipped when I saw how good she looked at the club for her uncles' birthday. Whoever the guy was that stepped in trying to defend her, was going to get what's coming to him. I know all about his deadly hands, so the best approach to get his ass, is to kill him. There's no way he's getting away with trying to take my girl and knocking me out in the club.

"What up?" My phone started ringing and interrupting me out of my thoughts. It was my boy Tony calling.

"I got the info you were looking for."

"Alright, send it to my phone."

"Yo, I got some bad news for you, too." I sat up in the

bed to give him my attention.

"What's up?"

"I just saw him drop shorty off at home, and they were all over each other. From the looks of it, he is fucking her." The hairs on the back of my neck stood up when he said that.

"Alright. Good looking out." I threw some clothes on and jumped in my car. The possibility of someone else pleasing her was clouding my mind. I almost had two accidents on the way. I picked my phone up when I was outside.

"What Tristan?"

"Oh, that's how we speak to one another now?" I hadn't seen her in a few weeks, so I assume she still mad about me cursing at her after fucking.

"Tristan, I'm tired. What do you want?"

"Come outside. I need to talk to you."

"Right now?"

"Yea, right now."

"Give me a minute."

I sat in the car thinking about what I was going to say to her. I don't have the right to even question her, but fuck it, she owes me answers.

She came outside looking like she just got fucked and it made me angrier. I unlocked the door, and she slipped in.

"What's up?"

"Close the door."

"No. I'm not staying out long."

"Close the door, Cady." She got out and walked back to the house. I knew I couldn't act up too much, because she still lived at home. I took hold of her arm and stopped her.

"What?" She yelled. Her mom opened the door to see if she was ok. She told her she could go back in. I moved her to the side for more privacy.

"You fucking that nigga?" She didn't even have a reaction.

"Tristan, is this why you called me out here?"

"Answer my question."

"For what? If I give you an answer, what is that going to do?"

"I thought we were getting back together." She threw her head back laughing.

"You can't be serious."

"Listen, bitch. Just because some nigga taught you how to fuck doesn't mean shit. You're still that same pathetic girl trying to be loved."

"Tristan, there's no need for you to be mean to me. I don't want to be with you anymore." Is this bitch really saying we're over?

"What? Ypu in love iwht that nigga?" She smiled and put her head down.

"This right, she's in love with me." I was shocked, when I heard his voice, because I didn't hear him pull up.

"What you doing over here baby?" She asked stepping around me. I turned around, and he bent down to kiss her. I snatched her arm back to get her away from him.

"Your mom called and said this dumb nigga was out here bothering her daughter; *my* girl." I continued to pull her arm.

"Tristan, get off of me." He stepped to me, and before I knew it, he had me hemmed up against the house. This nigga was definitely head over heels about her already.

"Stop, Rory. That's enough."

"You're protecting him?" He sounded aggravated.

"No. I just don't want you to get in trouble. Come on.
Let him go. Please." He looked into her eyes and let me go.

"Get the fuck outta here." He yelled out, grabbed her
hand, and they started walking off. I pulled the gun out my
waist and aimed it straight at him.

BOOM! BOOM!

"Noooooo!" It all happened so fast.

I aimed it at him, but she jumped in front of him and
was hit. I ran to my car and peeled out. It's fucked up she got
caught in the crossfire but if I can't have her, neither will he.

<u>Chanel</u>

I was at work when I noticed Miles calling my phone back-to-back. I didn't care to speak to him, so I shut it off. Twenty minutes later, he comes storming inside my job looking like a mad man. I was behind the register helping customers, and praying he didn't act up.

After the last person left, I came around and moved right past him. I hadn't spoken to him since his ex came in my store.

"Yo, why you shut your phone off?" I continued to ignore him until I felt him right behind me.

"What Miles?"

"You're standing over here giving me an attitude when your best friend in the hospital fighting for her life."

"What are you talking about? I only have one best friend, and I just spoke with her an hour ago."

"Yea, well she was shot outside her house." I swear the air just left my body when he said that. I grabbed onto the shelf to keep from falling.

"Come on, Chanel. We have to get to the hospital." I sat

on the floor with my knees in my chest praying to God he

didn't just say why I thought he said. I heard my manager ask

what happened when he walked up. Miles explained to him the

story and that's the last thing I heard. Miles carried me to the

car and sped to the hospital.

When I walked in, I saw Cady's mom, dad, her uncle,

Donovan, Rory, and his sister. I turned around, and two other

older couples came towards us. I found out they were Rory and

Miles' parents, who all seemed to know one another through

Donovan.

"Rory, are you ok?" He was sitting with his head down

and his hands over his head. There was blood all over his

clothes and some on his hands. He looked up with tears in his

eyes, and that's when I knew he was in love with Cady.

"She's going to be ok." I tried to remain calm myself.

"Nah, there was so much blood. I'm going to kill that

motherfucker." He yelled out and tried to get up. His dad and

the other guys took him outside to calm down. I gave her mom a hug and listened to her tell me what happened. I couldn't believe Tristan did that.

"If anything happens to her, Rory is going to tear this town up looking for him." His sister, Angel, said shedding a few tears herself.

"Why do you say that?" I asked being nosy. I knew he just told her he was in love with her, but he wasn't a killer.

"Because Tristan is a Crip, and Rory is a Blood. Tristan just woke up the beast in my brother and started a war." My eyes shot open when she said that. Why wasn't anyone as shocked as me? I looked over at Cady, Rory, and Miles' mom who all nodded at what she said.

"Wait. So you're telling me Rory and Miles are Bloods?" I was now more pissed finding that out. I didn't do gangbangers, and neither did Cady. *There's no way she knew and didn't tell me. She has to get away from him.* I thought to myself.

The doctor came walking up a few minutes later. The guys were still outside somewhere so Angel went to get them.

"Mrs. Simms." We all pointed to her mom.

"Yes."

"Hi, I'm Doctor Johnson. Can you have a seat?" We all sat down and listened.

"It was touch and go with your daughter at first but she is very strong. She was shot in the chest and abdomen." Her mom pasped.

"There were no major organs hit, which is a good thing. Unfortunately, she was a couple weeks pregnant and with the amount of blood loss, she lost the baby." Just as he said it, Rory walked up. The look on his few said it all. Not only was she shot, but his baby died in the process.

"WHAT!!!!!!" Rory yelled, hemming the doctor up against the wall.

"Let him go. I understand you're mad, but let him go." Rory's dad was in his face.

"I'm sorry, Doc. We didn't know, and that would've been his first child."

"I understand." He finished telling us she was in recovery and high off the medications. We probably wouldn't be able to see her until tomorrow.

"Rory are you ready?" His mom asked.

"I'm not leaving."

"Rory you need to get cleaned up. She doesn't need to see you like this."She said rubbing his back.

"Mom, I'm not leaving."

"Listen baby, I know you're hurting, but we are all hurting right now. That was my first grand baby, and from what you told me today, the girl you were in love with. Do you think she would want you coming in with all her blood on you reminding her of what happened?" He looked at her.

"Miles will take you home to get cleaned up, and then, if you want to come back, fine." The way his mom spoke to him in a peaceful yet stern voice made him get up.

"Are you staying?" He asked me.

"Yes. I'm not going anywhere."

"Donovan, who else is staying? The only way I'm leaving is if someone stays here with Chanel to protect her. I can't take a chance of leaving, and he comes up here."

"Miles, can you stay?" He asked him. Miles shook his head and gave him a man hug.

"I'll be back. Please don't let anything else happen to her."

"You know I won't. Just go get yourself together and hurry back so you can see her when she wakes up." Angel left with him as well. Me, Miles and her parents stayed.

"Are you ok, Chanel?" He asked and wrapped his around me.

"Yea. I'm ok now that I know she's ok." He wiped my eyes with his hands.

"She's going to be alright." He rubbed my back and lifted my head. He placed a kiss on my lips and smiled.

****

We stayed in the hospital all night with Rory. When she woke up, her parents were the first to see her, and when they came out to get Rory, he couldn't move.

"What's the matter?" I asked him.

"I can't see her like that. Can you tell her I'm out here,

but I can't see her now?"

"HELL NO!! Rory get up and go see her." He was pissing me off. He looked at me, then at Miles who shrugged his shoulders and went inside. We all watched him go in the room and a few minutes, later he came storming out.

"I'm out yo." Rory came out wiping his eyes. Everybody looked confused as hell. Her mom and I ran back there to see what happened. The nurse blocked the door and told us when he came back there he couldn't take seeing her like that. As if things couldn't get any worse, some bitch caught him at the elevators.

"Are you ok? Oh my God, I heard it was you that got shot." She hugged and kissed him, and he stood there staring at her like she was crazy.

"Who the fuck are you?" She let go and looked at me.

"I'm his girl, who are you?"

"That's funny, because I thought his girl was my best friend. Rory what's going on?" I stood there tapping my foot and waiting for an answer.

"Do you want to tell her? Or should I?"

"Taylor, I'm not doing this right now with you." He tried to push her away.

"Oh, but you are Rory. You see, my best friend just got shot trying to protect your ass. Then, she lost her baby and almost died again, only for this bitch to come up in here saying she's your girl too. So somebody better tell me what the hell is going on." Miles was looking at me shaking his head.

"I told Taylor this morning Cadence was my girl when she stopped by. Taylor is more than my girl; she's my wife. I was just avoiding her, so I didn't have to tell Cadence." I tried to swing off on him, and Miles grabbed me.

"Ok, Miles. I'm calm." He finally let me go and I walked over to Rory.

"Ok, you're telling me you have two women you're in love with?" When he didn't respond, I couldn't do anything but walk away.

"Don't say anything to her Chanel." He yelled and I turned around.

"I am not going to break her heart." I shook myhead.

"She lost her baby and almost her life all in one day

over a no good ass nigga. I'm going to say this to you one time and one time only. STAY THE FUCK AWAY FROM HER." I shouted the last part.

"I don't care how much she request to see you or call, you stay away from her. When she is better and can handle it, then you can bring your trifling ass back around to break the news. Until then, you and your wife need to get the fuck outta here."

I stayed at the hospital for a few hours before I went home to change. All that happened today was crazy and I needed a break.

I was getting out the shower and heard a knock at my door. I looked through the peephole and blew my breath before opening it. This was going to be a long night.

Miles

"I thought Chanel was going to kill your ass in there." I looked over at my boy in the passenger side with his head back and eyes closed.

"Man, I know she's going to tell her." I kind of felt bad for him, because I knew how he felt about Cadence, but I also kept telling him he needed to tell her.

"Nah, bro. You know I got you. I'm going over there after I drop you off." He shook his head laughing.

"Nigga, she hasn't fucked with you like that since Tory blew your spot up at her job."

"I know right. She's stubborn as hell, but I got something for her ass tonight. I'm giving her some of this act right when I get there. Mark my words; she about to be all over a nigga." He got out the car laughing, and I pulled off to go see Chanel.

"Open the door." I told her when I heard her walking and look through the peephole.

"What?" She said snatching the door open.

"Listen, don't be mad at me. I don't have anything to do with it." I pushed my way past her. She locked the door and went in her room. When she didn't come back out, I went to check on her.

"Yes, he was up there, Cady. He has some things to handle. I'm sure he'll be back. Ok, love you, too, girl. I'll talk to you tomorrow." I stood at the door listening to her conversation.

"So, she's awake?"

"Yea. She woke up not too long after that asshole left."

"Did you tell her?" She rolled her eyes and pulled her sweat pants up.

"No. I should; but I'm not, because I won't be the one that's going to break the news to her. I can't believe he did some shit like that."nShe was still angry.

"What do you mean?"

"If he was married, he should've told her. He just told her he was in love with her; yet, he left out one major detail, which is, he had a wife."

"Yea, you're right. At least, she's ok now." I sent a message to Rory saying she wouldn't tell Cadence.

"I'm not going to say anything, but you tell him I said, he better not take his ass to the hospital or accept any of her calls or all hell is going to break loose." I sent him the message and put my phone on the dresser. I put my hands around her waist and pulled her close.

"Let go Miles. We don't get down like that."

"Girl, you know you're mine." She threw her head back laughing.

"Ugh. You have Tory for that."

"I'm not with her. I haven't seen her in a few months."

"Yea, ok." I picked my phone back up, called Tory, and put her on speaker. She answered on the third ring.

"What's up, Miles? It's been a long time."

"Yea, I know. How long has it been?"

"I don't know, maybe three or four months." I saw the smirk on Chanel's face.

"You coming over or what?"

"About that. I was just calling to tell you I'm with

someone now, so don't call my phone anymore."

"I hope it isn't that low budget Rite Aid bitch." Chanel's face turned up.

"Don't let me hear out in the streets that you said anything to her, or put your hands on her."

"Whatever. You'll be back. You always come back." She laughed.

"Nah, not this time." I hung the phone up and made Chanel sit on my lap. She sat with her arms folded but grinning hard as hell.

"You didn't have to do that."

"Yes I did, or I would never hear the end of it." I let my hands slide up and down the top part of her legs.

"So, I'm your girl now?"

"Yup."

"Don't I get a say-so in it?"

"Nope. Bring those lips to me." I parted her lips with my tongue, and we went at it for a few minutes. This was going to be our first time together sexually and I'm about to get it in so we went in the bedroom.

I pulled the shirt over her head and sucked on each breast going back and forth to make sure each one got the same amount of attention. As I did, she put my hand down her pants so I could feel how wet she was. I had her step outta them, I laid back on the bed and told her to position herself on my face.

"Fuck Miles; this feels so good." She rocked her pussy on my face and had two orgasms back-to-back.

"I got something for you." She said taking my pants and boxers off.

"That looks delicious." I sat up on my elbows and watched her work her jaw muscles. The way she sucked and slurped had a nigga falling in love.

"Damn, girl. Suck that shit." I saw her hand move in between her legs.

"Nah. That's my job." I had her stand up and we performed in a 69 position. The way she cupped my balls had me tensing up. I had to stop eating her pussy, because she was sucking the hell out of it.

"Shit, Chanel. I'm about to cum."

"Mmmmm hmmm. Cum in my mouth, baby. I want to

taste you." I had to hold onto the sheets, I came so hard. She made sure to get everything out too.

I made her stay on top to catch my breath and went back to feasting on her. I stuck one finger in her ass while I bit gently down on her clit.

"Miles. I'm cummmming." She screamed and dug her nails in my leg.

My dick was hard again, and I wanted to feel the inside of her. I pulled her to the edge of the bed, spread her legs open and pushed my way in with no mercy. She wanted to be stubborn; I was about to give her this act right.

"Miles don't stop. Oh God, don't stop. It feels so good." I fucked her all night in so many different positions. We tapped out at the same time from being drained.

"Shit girl, I can't front, I thought you would've been tapped out."

"Nope. I know how to hang." She looked up at me and pecked my lips.

"Hell yea, you do. So, you my girl now or what?"

"I guess."

"Oh, you guess?" I watched her go in the bathroom to start the shower.

"You know you're my man. Come take a shower with me, but we're not fucking, because I'm tired." I moved the blankets off my leg and jumped in with her. We washed each other up, and minutes later, we were both knocked out.

<u>Tristan</u>

"Yo, please tell me it wasn't you who tried to kill Rory and ended up shooting Donovan's niece." I put my head down, as I listened to Mace go in on me. Mace was my uncle who ran the Crips out here and a few other states. He didn't have as much clout as Donovan, but he was still respected and made money just the same.

"She stepped in front of him." I honestly told him.

"FUCK Tristan. Do you know what you just did?"

"What are you getting mad for? Fuck that nigga." He got in my face and scoffed up a laugh.

"You just started a fucking war with niggas we been trying to keep on our good side. And for what? Some chick that didn't want your ass no more, because you kept cheating on her."

"I wasn't cheating on her. She needed help in the bedroom, so I had some of my female friends join in." The other guys in there were shaking their heads.

"Listen to how dumb you sound. Who brings other bitches in the bedroom with their main chick?" he chuckeld.

"You better hope… better yet, nigga, you better pray they only come looking for you." He took the shot he had on his desk.

"Why you say that?"

"Bro, we've been keeping the peace for years with them, and here you are trying to kill one of the most notorious ones. Do you know that nigga can kill you with his bare hands if he wants to? If you don't know about him, you better ask around. He one ain't to be fucked with, and now you shot the niece of the man that runs the entire East Coast *Bloods*. What the fuck were you thinking?"

"You make it seem like we don't have our own people."

"Tristan, you're not hearing me." He came over to me.

"You are one of us, and yes we will have your back, but you tried to get at a nigga over petty shit. No one wants to get involved to help your ass. A lot of people are about to die because of you, and you don't even give a fuck."

"Ain't nobody going to die." He hemmed me up by my

shirt, and the two guys in the office stood up and pointed their guns at my head.

"Nigga, every last one of us has a family, and you just put a bounty on all of us. You better act like you fucking care before I have one of them take your dumb ass out. Figure this shit out." He let go and nodded his heads for them to put their weapons away.

"How am I supposed to do that?" He shook his head and laughed.

"Get the fuck out of my office, yo. I'm sick of looking at you." I sucked my teeth and headed to the door.

"If I hear you're out there talking reckless about what went down, or you're going back after Rory or the girl, I will kill your ass myself and my sister will be buying that black dress."

I walked out his office mad as hell. Who did he think he was telling me what to do? I'm a grown ass man. I pressed the alarm on my car, and before I could sit down, someone lit my car up with bullets. I dove underneath one of the other cars, because my tires were flat, and I couldn't get under it. It seemed like the shooting went on forever. I heard two niggas laughing and talking.

"Did you see that nigga face?"

"Yea, he talks all that shit, and his punk ass ran. He better hope we find him before Donovan does." I heard the car door shut and waited a few minutes before I got up. I saw my uncle, the two guys from the office, and a few others standing around.

"Come here stupid." My uncle yelled out to me. I wiped the dirt off my clothes and went to see what he wanted.

"This is only the beginning." He handed me a sheet of paper I saw him take off the windshield. *It read: "There's nowhere to hide. We're coming for you, so tell your mom to get that black dress out."*

"I'm not worried."

"Take this stupid motherfucker to my condo. I'm about to make some calls to see if we can dead this shit. I'm not about to let people die over you." Two dudes snatched me up and threw me in a van like I was the enemy. To them, I guess I was. What the fuck did I get myself into?

Cadence

It's been three weeks since my ex shot me and I haven't seen or heard from Rory yet. Everyone keeps telling me it's because he's hurting too. *Excuse me, I'm the one who was shot.* Chanel promised to drive me over to the gym to see him. She said Miles told her he was there.

When we pulled up, I immediately, got butterflies in my stomach. I missed him so much and hoped he felt the same. We walked into his office, and he and Miles were eating lunch.

"Hey Cadence. How are you?" Miles spoke first. I couldn't even speak. Rory and I just stared, as if we were the only two people in the room.

"Let's go so they can talk."

"Hell no. I'm sitting right here." Chanel must've known something was up, because this wasn't like her.

Rory walked around his desk and hugged me so tight, I had to push him away a little. I was still in some pain, but I needed to see him. He pecked my lips and told me to take a seat.

"You look good baby." I smiled and started blushing. I heard Chanel suck her teeth. Just then, that same chic Taylor, who was at his house came through the door.

"Why is she here?" Taylor sat back in his office chair and made herself comfortable.

"We have to go through this again. What the fuck, Rory?" She sassed and rolled her eyes.

"Listen Cadence, is it? He and I are married, so any chance you thought you had with being together is gone." I snatched my hand back from his and felt the tears starting to fall.

"Shut the fuck up Taylor. Why you even here?" He yelled at her.

"Please tell me she''s not your wife." When he put his head down, it was the confirmation I needed to get up and leave. I saw my girl getting her stuff.

"Let me explain." He tried to talk.

"No need."

"Please Cadence."

"Don't beg her Rory. Who cares of she's mad?"

"SHUT THE FUCK UP TAYLOR." He screamed making everyone jump.

"Cadence."

"It all makes sense to me now. The reason why you couldn't give yourself to me; the reason she was in your office, and why she popped up at your house. How could you not tell me you were married? A girlfriend, I may be able to swallow, but a wife. Why does bad shit keep happening to me? I mean, do I deserve this?" I stood there, with tears streaming down my face.

"No you don't Cadence. I'm sorry you found out this way and I wanted to tell you, but I didn't know how."

"You didn't know how. You should've found a way before I took two bullets for your ass and lost my baby that I didn't even know was in my stomach. This is because I left Tristan, isn't it?" I looked up like I was speaking to God.

"If I stayed with him, this would've never happened. FUCK, I'm so stupid." He tried reaching out for me, but I smacked his hands away.

"Cadence, don't leave." I laughed and looked at Taylor who was soaking everything in.

"Chanel, can you take me home please?" She had a few tears in her eyes too.

"Rory, I know you said you needed time to tie up a few loose ends, but now you can take all the time you need." I turned to the woman.

"Taylor, woman-to-woman, I apologize for sleeping with your husband. As you can see, I was unaware." Chanel draped her arm around me and walked out with me.

"Cadence." He yelled out. I turned around to see what he wanted.

"What?"

"I love you." I rolled my eyes and sucked my teeth.

"Goodbye Rory." I shut the door, and before we could pull off, Miles came to speak to Chanel. I wanted to leave before Rory came to the car, but it was too late.

"I'm sorry Cadence, but this isn't what it seems. If you just let me explain." I put my hand up.

"I don't want to talk about it, Rory. I am not a home

wrecker."

"Cadence, you can't wreck a home that's already knocked down."

"How could you? I just told you I was in love with you."

"Cadence, I still wanna be with you and I love the hell outta you." He wiped the tears from my eyes, as I let my head fall back on the seat.

"This is it for us. It was fun while it lasted. Thanks for teaching me how to satisfy a man in the bedroom." I knew that would piss him off.

"Don't play with me. I better not hear you're out here fucking anyone."

"Are you serious? Can we please go Chanel? The pain is becoming unbearable." I wasn't sure what hurt worse; his betrayal, or from being shot. Chanel turned the car on, kissed Miles, and pulled off.

<u>Rory</u>

"FUCK!!!! Taylor why in the hell would you tell her that? You know I was trying to give her time to heal."

"Who cares? Now that she's out of our lives, we can get this marriage back to where it used to be."

"Taylor, you just don't get it. You and I will never be like we used to."

"Don't say that Rory. You know how much I love you." She got up out the chaor and tried ot rub her hand down my chest and I moved them away.

"Taylor, we were young when we got married, and once you slept with DeShawn, any chance of me ever loving you again went out the window."

"It was a long time ago. Why can't you get past it?"

I thought about what she just asked me. Could I get past it, or was it that I didn't want to because I was now in love with someone else? I remember that day like it was yesterday.

Taylor and I met a few months before I went to jail on a

gun charge. She claimed to have fallen in love with me and wanted to be my ride or die chick. She said we should get married, so if anything happened, they couldn't make her testify. Me, not thinking, thought it was a good idea. We got our marriage license, stood in front of the mayor, and boom, it was a done deal.

A few months later, I was sentenced and sent to away to what they call "The Gladiator" jail down in Bordentown, NJ. I was only down for a few months when I started hearing stories about Taylor and my dude DeShawn I used to roll with. Rumor had it, they were fucking and living as if they were a couple. She still came to visit faithfully, and I let her believe we had a chance when I came home.

When I was released, I didn't tell her because I knew she was lying. My mom came with my sister to get me, because my dad couldn't get off work.

Anyway, I borrowed my moms' car that night and went to Deshawn's house. Low and behold, when he opened the door, she was laying on the couch in a robe, and he only had on a pair of sweats.

I beat the shit out of him and told her to stay away from me. Ever since the, she basically stalked me, and I would hit it now and then, but I was done with her. I never even thought about us still being married until the night I met Cadence.

I had a sit down with my dad, and he told me, if I want to move forward with any female, I had to deal with my past. He called his lawyer over, and we had divorce papers drawn up and served to Taylor. She refused to sign them and to this day, she still won't.

The shit she pulled at the hospital by screaming it out made me want to kill her. Then, she tried to hurt Cadence even more by being the first to tell her. I don't know why Taylor was doing this, because she knows it over.

"Taylor, can you please sign the papers?" I attempted to be nice.

"No. You can ask me a thousand times, and I will keep saying the same thing. You're not leaving me."

"Nothing you do is going to make me want you. The love is gone, and even though I slipped a few months ago and fucked you, I still feel the same. I don't want you anymore."

She stormed out the office crying, and Miles just shook his head.

"Yo. You got some serious shit going on."

"Don't I know it?"

"What are you going to do?"

"Man, I don't know. Can you call Chanel and see where Cadence is?" He took his phone out, and when he told me she was home, I flew over there.

****

"What happened?" Her mom asked, when she opened the door. I explained everything to her.

"I don't like what you did to my daughter. However; you make her smile, and she started getting her self-esteem back when she's around you. That man scarred her emotionally and mentally and now, you just did the same thing."

"I know. I didn't mean to fall in love with her, but I couldn't help it."

106

"I know; she told me what you did for her." She smirked.

"Huh?"

"Huh? My ass. My daughter tells me everything. Listen, she is upstairs lying down. I can't tell you she's not hurting, but maybe if you explain to her what is really going on, she'll listen. I'm going to run out to the store, and I'll be back." I went upstairs to Cadence room and found her asleep.

I pulled a chair in front of the bed and watched her sleep. She was so beautiful, as I sat and watched her breath in and out. I moved the hair out of her face, and her eyes popped open.

"Rory. What are you doing here?" She moved the covers back and went to the bathroom. I sat there waiting for her to come out. She laid in the bed and put the covers on her. I took my shoes and shirt off and got in behind her.

"Boy, get up." She tried to push me out the bed.

"Not until you listen to me." She turned on her side, put her head on arm, and stared at me.

"What?"

"I don't know where to start."

"How about you start by telling me why you didn't mention your wife." I laid back and told her my entire life story. She didn't have a reaction even when I told her I was gang affiliated. She waited for me to finish before she spoke.

"Well, aren't you the little bad boy?" She laughed and laid back. I climbed on top of her gently.

"I love you, Cadence. I don't want what happened to make you lose faith in what I promised you. There's nothing I won't do to have you in my life and keep you safe." I kissed her lips, and she slipped her tongue in. I was shocked, but I accepted it. She pushed me off her body and pulled her pajamas down.

"Just fuck me. I need to feel you inside me right now." I looked at her like she was crazy.

"No."

"What do you mean no?"

"Cadence, I want to make love to you but not like this."

"Rory, I don't want you to make love to me. I just want you to fuck me. Please, my body is aching for you right now."

She put her fingers inside her pussy, then in my mouth. I tried

so hard to resist her, but I couldn't. I stripped out my clothes

and entered my safe haven inside of her. She was so wet.

"This feels good, Rory. Oh God, I needed this." She put

her legs on my shoulder and begged me to go deeper.

"Cadence, promise you won't give my pussy away."

"I promise." She moaned in my ear.

"You're pussy is like my drug. I don't want you giving

anyone else a fix."

"I'm not baby." She got on top and took control. She

threw her head back and pinched her nipples. I massaged her

clit and watched her bite down on her lip. The scene before me

was so exotic that she had me cumming quick.

"I'm cumming, Cadence. Fuck, here I come." She

ground faster and came with me.

"I want some more Rory."

"Really?"

"You said this was my dick before, and I could have it

anytime I want. Did you change your mind?" I shook my head

no and brought her face to mine. We went at it for another hour until we heard her mom yelling up the steps.

"I love you, Rory."

"I love you, too. Do you want me to leave?" I asked, watching her put clothes on.

"No. Can you stay with me? I don't want you to leave." I pulled her close, and she rested her head on my chest.

"I'm not ever leaving you."

<u>Chanel</u>

I felt bad for my girl when she went to see Rory, and the dumb bitch Taylor came in throwing shade. Cadence called and told me how he came to her house and explained everything to her, but I told her to still be careful. Anyone in their right mind can see Taylor is not backing down without a fight, but if a fight is what she wants, she fucking with the right two bitches. Cady and I aren't anything to fuck with.

I was putting on my uniform for work, when I heard what sounded like glass breaking. I look out my window, and this bitch was standing there with a grin on her face. I had to calm myself down before I went outside and caught a charge. I dialed Miles' number on the way down the steps.

"Hey baby, what's up? Are you on your way to work yet?" His voice was sexy as hell over the phone.

"Miles, I hope you have bail money for me, because I'm about to catch a charge."

"Wait, wait. Chanel, what's going on?" I opened the

door with him still on the phone trying to get me to answer him.

"Tory, I see you need that ass beat again." I taunted.

"Bitch you ain't beating nobody ass." She locked her door, but kept the window rolled down just enough so I could hear her.

"Get out the damn car then." I grabbed the handle, and it was locked.

"Leave Miles alone, or this won't be the last time you see me." She yelled out the window and pulled off.

I could hear him on the phone yelling, but I just disconnected the call. I don't have time for this shit right now. They just promoted me to assistant manager, which is paying me four extra dollars an hour; a bitch doesn't have time to be late.

I called for an Uber to pick me up because this chick flattened all my tires and busted out my back window. Miles got some good ass dick, but damn, I am not about to be fighting over it.

I saw Miles pulling in the driveway and pressing my doorbell on the outside door. I didn't say two words as the driver pulled off.

I clocked in, put my purse and keys in my locker, and sat in my office. Yes, a bitch had her own office, desk, computer, and all that manager shit. I may work at Rite Aid, and that's ok; a bitch is not about to depend on a man to take care of her. Shit, look at how that dumb bitch Tory acting because he cut her off.

There was a knock at my door, as I turned on my computer to get the schedules done for next week. It was one of the cashiers from the front telling me someone was looking for me. I knew it was Miles, and I didn't feel like being bothered, so I had her tell him I was in a meeting. I watched her go back up front and relay the message. He left the store, and I finished doing the schedules.

An hour before I got off, Cady sent me a message asking me to have some drinks at the bar. I told her I had to run home to change, but I would pick her up around seven. It was Thursday, and everyone know it's ladies' night at the bar. We were about to get free drinks all night.

I got off at five and forgot my car was fucked up, so I

had Cady pick me up, and told her, she could get dressed at my house.

She pulled in the driveway, and I noticed all my tires were fixed and my window was also. I didn't even bother to say thank you to Miles, because as I see it, it was his fault this shit happened.

"I thought you said your car was messed up?"

"It was this morning. I guess he came by and fixed it. I mean, it was his ex that did it; it's the least he could do."

"Yea. You're right. Let's go inside, so we can pregame before we go, just in case there's some cheap ass niggas in there." We high-fived one another and walked inside. I opened my door and saw roses in my kitchen, living room, and bedroom. There was a note on my bed.

Chanel,

I'm sorry you keep getting caught up in my ex's shit. I want you to know there's nothing going on with us. You are the only woman I'm with, and I'm not trying to let you go. I hope you like the flowers I got

Miles

"Ugh, how did he know we were going out?" Cady turned her head with a grin on her face.

"I may have told Rory."

"You may have or you did?" I questioned.

"I did. I'm sorry, Chanel. You didn't tell me everything when I spoke to you. You just said your car wasn't working."

"Fuck it. I'm sure he'll be doing his own thing later anyway. I'll see him tomorrow. Let's get ready."

Miles

I don't know what the fuck Tory was thinking going over to Chanel's house. One would believe I was still fucking with her by the way she flattened all her tires and bust the windows out her car. Tory is on some petty shit.

I called my boy who works for a towing company to get the tires changed, then I called safe light to get the windshield fixed.

I was definitely feeling Chanel and the way her pussy was set up, I wasn't trying to allow another nigga to slide up in there. I picked her up a few dozens of roses and paid the manager of her apartment complex to let me in to leave them. I left her a note apologizing because I know she was mad.

I went by Donavan's house afterwards, because he wanted to call a meeting with us over that dumb nigga Tristan. When I got there, Rory was standing outside with a few other bloods. I got out the car and a few black Yukons pulled up with tinted windows. No one knew who it was so we walked up to them with our guns drawn.

"Ok. I see." Donovan was talking on the phone when he came out the door.

"Stand down." He told all of us. We backed up still being cautious.

One of the doors opened and out stepped Mace. All of us drew our weapons again, but this time, his people got out and did the same. I could see right now there was going to be some shit.

"D. What's going on my man?" Mace and him gave each other a hug like they haven't seen one another in years.

"Ah, maintaining man. Come on in, so we can talk." He walked in with about ten of his men. We sat out in the backyard with them on one side and us on the other, ice grilling each other.

"What brings you here Mace?" Donovan handed him a drink and sat down.

"Well, I'm here on my nephew's behalf. I heard what happened, and as much as I want to say fuck him like I would anyone else, my sister won't allow it."

"You're sister. How is Patrice doing?" He had a sneaky ass grin on his face.

"She's good. But enough about her. What can we do to resolve this?"

"Not a damn thing. He signed his death certificate when he tried to kill me, but got my girl instead." He turned around, when Rory stepped in the room. He was on the phone when we first came out here.

"You must be Rory."

"I am and there's nothing you can do or say to save him."

"I see. If I'm not mistaken Rory, you stole his girl from him and knocked him out at Donovan's party, so it appears you started this." Rory shook his head laughing.

"He got knocked out in the club for trying to put his hands on her, and then talking shit. I got over that, but when he tried to take my life and missed; he ended up taking my kids' life. Would you allow a nigga to breathe if he did that to you?" Rory was in his face now.

"Ok, Rory. I think he understands his nephews' days

are numbered." I didn't want any bloodshed over Donovan's house. Even though he would understand; this was supposed to be a sit-down.

"What kid?" Mace asked confused.

"She was pregnant. Oh, Tristan didn't tell you that?" Donovan was now getting pissed off.

"Nah, he didn't tell me that. Listen, what else can we do to try and resolve this?" Mace was still trying to get him to change his mind.

"Nothing. I don't even know why you're here. That nigga should be here begging for his life with his punk ass. Just tell him I'm coming for him." Rory said and walked out.

I followed behind him, because it was evident he was ready to go looking for him. We were walking out when Cadence came in the house. He tried to hide his anger but she caught on.

"Hey baby. What's wrong?" He hugged her. Mace and his boys came out the back with Donovan not too far behind. They all stopped when they saw her.

"So you're the infamous Cadence."

"Who are you?" she sassed with much attitude.

"This is Tristan's uncle. He came here on behalf of his nephew to try and resolve what he did." Donovan chimed in and gave her a kiss on the cheek. Cadence stepped away from Rory but stayed close enough to still be in his presence.

"Mace is it?"

"Yes, beautiful." I could see Rory getting mad by the way he was looking her up and down.

"It's a shame that in all of four years, I've never met you or half your family, when Tristan and I were together. It would've been nice to meet you." She smiled.

"I'm sorry you wasted your time coming here." He gave her a confused look. I was wondering why she didn't recognize him if he's Tristan's uncle.

"What do you mean?"

"I'm saying Tristan and I were over for a while when he decided to try and kill my man. Instead, he got me and my unborn child, who you can see wasn't so lucky. Whatever my man, my uncle and all of them have planned for him, he deserves it."

"I'm sorry you feel that way. I hate to think this war is starting over a woman."

"No, this war, as you call it, started because your nephew couldn't keep his dick in his pants. Your nephew was jealous and mad, because I didn't want him anymore. Therefore, another man stepped in and took his spot." She turned to Rory.

"I must say, he takes his job very serious when it comes to me."

"If that's what you believe." She scoffed up a laugh.

"Believe this Mace. Your nephew is going to get what's coming to him courtesy of my man. When the job is finished, I'm going to fuck him so good with no regrets of him taking your nephew's life. Now, if you'll excuse me, I have to go." She kissed my boy and went to the back.

"She's a feisty one, D. Too bad this is going to end up bad for her." Rory had the gun pressing on Mace's temple before he got the last word out. Before I knew it, Rory hit him so hard, two of his teeth flew out. It was total chaos in the house until we heard a gunshot.

"Get the fuck out." Cadence was standing there

pointing the gun at Mace, and Donovan's maids and butler had a gun pointing to some of the other guys.

"This ain't over." Mace yelled, as he and his boys walked out the house. I knew this shit was going to get out of hand. His maids and butler were no joke.

Donovan always said anyone that came in his house or worked in it should be aware of how to use a gun. I left not too long after. Shit, a nigga needed a drink and to climb up in some pussy.

Donovan

I was sitting in my office when my maid told me there was a woman waiting to speak to me. I thought it was my sister, but then again, her ass would just walk right in.

I backed my chair up from my desk and went to see who it was. She was in the living room with her back turned staring out one of the windows.

"Can I help you?" She turned around, and I had to adjust my dick. She stood there still looking as beautiful as ever.

Her medium brown skin was glowing against the sunlight. Her hair was swooped to the side with something holding it there. Her body was still just as I remembered; perfect. She stepped closer to me and wrapped her arms around my neck.

"It's been a long time, Donovan." She kissed my lips, letting some of her lip gloss rub off.

"Yes it has Patrice." She stepped back, and I put my

hand out offering her a seat.

Patrice and I dated years ago when Tristan was first born. No, he's not my son, but I did help her raise him the first few years of his life until I got locked up. She went back to his dad, which was fine, because she still came to visit, and the letters never stopped.

A drunk driver killed Tristan's dad one night. Patrice fell into a depression but ended up falling head over heels for the counselor who helped her through it. The year I was getting released, I was told she married another guy, so I never bothered her again, and now here she is.

"Patrice, you are looking as beautiful as ever. What do I owe the pleasure?"

"Donovan, I think we both know why I'm here."

"You're probably right, but I wanna hear it from you." She shifted in her seat before she spoke.

"Tristan." I got up, poured myself a drink from my minibar, and sat back down. I crossed my leg over the other and took a sip. I could tell I was making her uncomfortable by staring, but she is definitely the one that got away.

"What about Tristan?" I questioned.

"I need you to ask Christian's son, Rory, to squash this beef he has with him." I sat my cup on the table next to me and put my elbows on my knees.

"You know, I find it mighty funny that your son has you and his uncle coming over here on his behalf but he has yet to show his own face."

"Why would he show his face? So you guys can kill him? I'm begging you Donovan to call this off." I shook my head.

"Patrice, think about what you're asking me to do. My niece almost died that day; and she lost her baby. If she hadn't jumped in front of him, then Rory would've died."

"I understand Donovan, but he's my only son."

"I don't think you do Patrice. You know and have known, my niece is like my daughter. Your son had been treating her like shit for years, and I stayed out of it, because Cady wanted me to. Now you're asking me to stop the man that loves her, from killing him, when he almost killed her. Let me ask you this." She lifted her head up, and I saw the tears sliding down her face.

"If Rory tried to kill Tristan, shot his girl, and he lost the baby, would you have this same conversation with his family?" When she didn't answer, I knew she didn't care about my niece or the baby she lost.

"Get out Patrice."

"Donovan, please. I can't sleep at night knowing someone's trying to kill him." She tried to hug me, but I removed her hands.

"I couldn't sleep when I thought my niece was about to die."

"But she didn't." She said thinking that would make it better.

"No, but her baby did." She shut right up.

"The way you're over here begging for your son's life, and not giving a fuck about my niece or the loss of my great niece or nephew, shows me how ignorant and selfish you really are." I pointed to the door, but she didn't move.

"Selfish and ignorant. After all I did for you."

"What did you do for me, Patrice? Tell me." She put

her head down.

"Exactly. Nothing. You couldn't do the bid with me, which was fine, I get that, but then after your son's father died, you found someone else. Ok, I get that, but then, not only did you marry him, but you cut me off completely. When I tried to get at you, all your numbers were changed, and you sent a message through my sister not to contact you. Low and behold, that son of yours has a bounty on his head, and now, you want to come over here crying and asking for help. Get the fuck out before I toss your ass out." She snatched her stuff up off the couch and stormed to the door.

"I never stopped loving you Donovan. No matter who I'm with, my heart will always be with you."

"That's some shit you should've told me before all this happened and before you married someone else. Go ahead with that shit." I closed the door in her face, turned around and saw my sister standing there shaking her head.

"What?"

"Nothing D. You still love that woman."

"Well, even if I did, her son almost killed my niece and

murdered her baby. I don't have one ounce of remorse for what's going to happen to him. His uncle is going to get it too if he thinks he can walk up in here requesting a sit-down and then talk shit. I'm tired of all these motherfuckers." I went in my office and slammed the door. I knew she wasn't leaving, so I waited for the door to open.

"D. I kind of feel bad for her." I shot her the most evil look.

"Why is that?" I turned my laptop back on.

"That is her only son."

"Would you feel the same way if Cady didn't make it?" She put her head down, which gave me her answer.

"Look, I know it's a fucked up situation, but Tristan knew what he was doing when he went after Rory. Did he think Cady would get hurt? Probably not? But she did. Not only that; he still shot at Rory, and if you are going to pull your gun out, make sure you kill that motherfucker." She didn't say anything.

"What he should've done was kill Rory right after, but his bitch ass ran. He knew the consequences of his actions the minute he did it, because he ran straight to his uncle.”

“Do you think Rory is really going to kill him?” I smirked at her.

“Oh, he’s going to do more than kill him. He’s in love with Cady, and even though he has his own shit going on, he won’t allow anyone to bring harm to her. I don’t even think I could stop it if I wanted to. Rory has his mind set, and there’s nothing anyone can do to change it.”

“Do you think Cady can?” I looked at her.

“Look sis. I don’t think you should try and get involved at this point. Cady was here when his uncle came, and she made it very clear that she doesn’t care what Rory does to him.”

“Maybe I can talk her into asking him leave it alone.”

“You are as bad as Patrice.”

“Why?”

“Listen to yourself. You’re asking a mother and father of a child that was taken away from them because of a jealous ex, to forgive and forget like it never happened. Yes, they didn’t know about the baby, but that makes it worse. I’m asking you to stay out of it, because you're my sister. Cady is not going to take kindly to you asking her to do that after all he's done to her."

"You let me worry about Cady." She got up to leave.

"Ok, tell Cady to lock up when she comes in."

"What do you mean?"

"I mean when you go to her about this shit, she is going to flip, so just tell her what I said." She slammed the door when she walked out.

Fuck, I need a damn drink.

Cadence

The day Tristan's uncle came by to discuss squashing the beef, I was shocked at how fine he was. Yes, I was with my ex for years, but I never met his family. He always said it was just him and his mom and his uncle was never around, which I know now is a lie.

When I had the gun in my hand, I felt so powerful, I had Rory taking me to the gun range every other day just to get comfortable with using one. The two of us were now officially a couple everyone knew about and I wanted to celebrate again.

Chanel and I were on our way to the bar, because we were bored. The Tory shit wirh Miles aggravated Chanel and she claimed to be over him. He tried to make up with her over the last few weeks, but she was adamant about staying away. He even bought her roses and a new truck. She had no choice, but to take the roses because they were left in her house, but refused the truck.

"Damn, Chanel you wearing the hell out of that dress." She had on a tight bondage dress with some red bottoms to match. She had her hair up in a long ponytail, and her makeup was on point as usual.

I was wearing a white knee-length skirt with a black camisole top. I had on some Jimmy Choo's, and my hair was straight down. Chanel and I weren't rich, and even though we had on clothes from Macy's, we always made sure we had high-end shoes on. No one could tell what clothes we wore, but all bitches new the shoe game. If we weren't wearing red bottoms, they were Giuseppe's, Prada, Jimmy Choo's and the rest of the expensive ass ones.

We got to the club around ten, which is a bit early, but we didn't want a seat in VIP. We had more fun at the bar mingling and talking with the bartenders.

The bar started getting packed around twelve, and the DJ was getting it in on the turntables. Chanel and I were dancing on our bar stool when I felt someone push me and almost make me spill my drink.

"What the fuck?" I turned around, and it was the Taylor bitch with some busted looking chick.

"Oh. My bad; I didn't see you there." She gave a fake smile.

"Bitch. You saw me."

"You're right, I did see you. But that's what you get when you're sleeping with someone's husband."

"Wait, this is the bitch sleeping with Rory?" Her friend asked with her nose turned up. I could see Chanel put her drink down.

"Yup, that's me. The one and only, but let me ask you this. Did Taylor tell you, Rory's been asking for a divorce for a while now, and she won't give it to him?" Her friend must not have known, because she folded her arms up and looked at her.

"Girl, you know how Rory gets. All I have to do is fuck him, and he's over it."

"Yea, ok. That's why he's home waiting on me now right?" I saw how red her face got and her friend snickered.

"Ok bitch, you want to play. Let's play." Taylor said and I assumed she wanted to thow hands.

I got up off my stool getting ready to fight when she started clicking away on her phone.

"I tried to let you down easy since he can't seem to be the one to do it. Look at this." She passed me her phone, and it was a message she just sent to him asking if she could stop by and see him real quick, and he responded *yes*.

"That doesn't mean shit."

"Oh, no. I'm going to let you in on a little secret."

"What's that?" She pulled something out of her purse.

"I still have the key to his house. I'm going to give it to you, so you can witness what I'm going to do with your own eyes and then, you can leave us alone to fix our marriage."

"Ok, bet. I can't believe I'm going along with this." I shook my head.

"I will be at Rory's house in about an hour. If you can prove to me, you two are working on your marriage or even still sleeping together, I'll back off."

"Deal. Mandy, I'm going to drop you off at home and head over there." She shook her head in disgust at Taylor, as they headed for the door.

"Cady, are you sure you can handle this? I mean, if he told her to come over, it could only mean one thing at this time of night."

"You're right Chanel, but after everything we went through, I know he doesn't want to be with her." We had a few more drinks, and after 45 minutes, we headed to Rory's house.

"Do you think I should text him?"

"If he knows you're coming over already, there's no need to." I agreed with her, and we got in the car to leave. I had butterflies in my stomach the entire way over there. I prayed Rory wasn't sleeping with her, because I couldn't take another heartbreak.

There were a few lights on in his house, but still, it was fairly dark. Chanel came in with me for support. There was soft music playing and some beers on the counter. I walked up the steps and saw Taylor's clothes scattered on the floor to his bedroom. I knew she did that to be extra. The bedroom door was cracked, and you could see inside.

Chanel stood with her back against the wall, because she didn't want to see it, which was ok with me. I didn't want her to see my man's dick if it was out. I pushed the door

opened and almost passed out from the sight. Taylor was riding

the hell out of Rory, and he was enjoying it.

"Ride that shit, Taylor. Yea, just like that." I heard him

saying to her. She must've heard me, because she turned

around still on top and winked her eye at me. I just nodded my

head, shut the door, and grabbed Chanel. I left the key by

Taylor's purse and left. We ran to the car, and before I knew it,

tears flooded my eyes. I was hysterically crying.

"Cady, let's stay at a hotel tonight." Chanel said,

rubbing my back. I nodded my head and wiped my eyes. We

both grabbed clothes from our house and went to check in at

the Marriott. I sent a message to my mom that I was staying

out, and I locked up when I left.

****

The next day, we decided to stay at the hotel for the

remainder of the weekend and just hang out like we used to.

She called in sick, and they believed her. We shut our phones on Sunday, and I had twenty text messages from Rory. I knew

I had to let him know I was ok. Especially with all the shit

going on, I decided called and he answered on the second ring.

"Cady, where are you? Are you ok?"

"I'm fine Rory. I stayed out with Chanel."

"Why? I thought you were supposed to come stay with

me." I looked at my phone like he was crazy. I had him on

speaker so when he said that. Chanel rolled her eyes.

"Look Rory, I'm going to cut to the chase. I came by

the other night, and you were fucking Taylor, so for you to sit

on the phone and ask me why I didn't stay with you is asinine.

Anyway, I just called to let you know I was ok, and you and

Taylor can work on your marriage." The phone got silent, but I

could hear him breathing on the other end.

"Hello Rory. What's the matter? Cat got your tongue."

"Cadence."

"Don't fucking Cadence me motherfucker. I trusted you,

and you did it to me again."

"I don't even know what to say. I don't have an

explanation on why that shit happened with Taylor, but it did.

I'm sorry you walked in on that. She came over to discuss us working on our marriage and -."

"I don't care what she came over there for, you weren't supposed to fuck her. Would you like it if I invited Tristan over, husband or not, and you walked in on me riding his dick?"

"Cadence, don't fucking play with me. What I did was fucked up, but I swear to God you better not fuck no other nigga." I laughed hard in the phone.

"I know you didn't just come out your face and say some shit like that. Nigga please. This pussy right here no longer belongs to you. That's right. I'm going to find me a good man who's not married and can love me the way I need. Oh, and you can bet I'm going to fuck the shit out of him, thanks to you."

"Cadence, if I find out."

CLICK!

I hung the phone up on his ass. I was done crying over him. I've been through too much to continue fucking with a nigga who keeps running back to his wife.

"I'm proud of you, Cady."

"Yea, well it's hurting like hell right now. I'm not sure if I should have done that. Maybe, I should see if he's really sorry."

"Don't even think about it. You and I are going out to Elizabeth's tonight and see what kind of men they have up there. Shit, the both of us need to leave these no good ass dudes alone and find some real niggas. You down or what?" I nodded my head yes.

Rory kept calling my phone, and I let it go to voicemail. I wasn't worried about him or Miles finding us, because we both turned off the find my iPhone apps. We did not need them showing up there.

<u>Rory</u>

It has been over a month since Cadence caught me fucking Taylor again. I still don't know how she got in the house, but it doesn't matter now. I tried getting in contact with Cady, and every time I went by her mom's, she said she wasn't there. Then, her uncle would say she just left. It was as if she knew when I was coming, and she would get ghost.

Even though I still wanted to go through with the divorce, I continued sleeping with Taylorr. I know it was probably confusing things, but she was throwing it at me, so I took it every time.

Tonight was Taylor's birthday, and she wanted to eat at one of the restaurants I owned, because they always made her favorite. When we arrived, Miles was already there with his ex, Tory. I invited him, because Taylor wanted to go out afterwards, and she knew I'd probably ignore her. She and Tory met about a month ago when Cadence called it quits.

The waitress came and took our orders, and Miles and I were talking, while the girls were getting to know one another.

Outta the corner of my eye, I watched Cady step in wearing a blue wrap around dress that was too short if you asked me. Then, some dude and two other people came in right behind her. The two of them spoke as they walked by.

"Hey Miles and Rory." Cadence said and kept walking. She didn't even acknowledge Taylor or Tory. I thought Miles was going to jump out his seat when he saw Chanel.

"Out of all the fucking places to eat, why did they come here?" Tory bitched.

"Who the fuck cares? You're with Miles, and I'm with my husband." I noticed how she threw husband in there.

I sat there staring at Cadence, and I couldn't help but be mad at myself for fucking up. She appeared to be extremely happy with this dude. He moved her hair behind her ear and started kissing on her neck. My blood was boiling at this point.

"What the fuck Rory? Are you going to stare at her the entire time?" Taylor was getting loud at the table. I noticed Chanel and Cady get up to go in the bathroom. Taylor was so busy yelling she didn't, so I took the time to excuse myself. I waited for Cady to come out, and when she did, I snatched her up in the men's room.

"What are you doing?" I had her hemmed up against the wall. I heard Chanel whispering for me to open the door, so she could get out. I knew she didn't wanna cause a scene.

"I miss you, Cady." I was still kissing her neck, but my hands were sliding up her dress.

"I can't tell. You're still with your wife."

"I don't give a fuck about her. If I did, do you think I'd be in here with you?"

"Rory, move. I have to go back out there." She tried pushing me off.

"Are you giving my pussy away to that nigga?" I slid my hands in her panties. I could feel her becoming wet as I touched it.

"Rory, stop." I lifted her dress up, pulled her panties down, put my tongue on her pussy, and her knees buckled.

"Oh God, Rory. We can't be doing this."

"You want me to stop?" I stuck my fingers inside, and she exploded on impact. Her breathing had increased so much, she couldn't catch her breath. I latched on to her clit and made her cum again. Her clit had the heartbeat thing going on. I kissed her stomach and moved to her breasts, as she stood there allowing me to.

"Rory. Oh God, make me cum again baby." She moaned softly, but enough for me to hear her. I needed to feel inside her. I unbuckled my jeans, pulled my clothes down, and my dick sprung out like a jack in the box. I picked her up and wrapped her legs around my waist.

"Come on Cady. They're going to come back in a minute to check on us."

"I'm coming Chanel. Just give me a minute." She tried to say loud enough for her to hear.

"I missed my pussy Cady. I want you cum all over my dick."

"Fuck. I'm cumming baby. Don't stop." She said, as I pumped harder and faster. I felt the blood rushing to the tip, and I let go with no regrets of not having on a condom.

"Shit Cady. Your pussy is still the best."

"Fuck. That dick still loves me." She let her head rest on my chest.

"Hell yea, it does, and so do I." I put her down on the sink and washed in between her legs, and then, helped her down.

"Don't give my pussy away, Cady. I mean that shit."

"Rory, please. I know you're still fucking her, and while I may not be with anyone else, there's going to come a time when I will." She kissed me on the cheek and stepped out.

Chanel snatched her away and rolled her eyes at me. I didn't care; I just fucked my future baby mama. I looked in the mirror and smiled. I came in her on purpose. If I couldn't have her, she was going to be pregnant and have to at least deal with me. I was washing my hands when Miles walked in grinning.

"You fucked her, didn't you?"

"Why do you ask me that?" I smirked.

"Because she came out grinning and waved at Taylor. Then, when she sat down, she winked at me."

"Yea, that's my baby. Anytime I see her, I'm going to fuck her."

"You two funny as hell. If that's the case, you need to leave Taylor alone for real. You know the bitch ain't wrapped too tight, and neither is Tory." I was in a good mood for the rest of the night.

I dropped Taylor off at home, because even though I was fucking her, she wasn't staying the night. I pulled into my driveway, and Cady was standing on my porch.

"Is everything ok?" I ran over to her.

"Yes. Can you just open the door?" I opened it and before I could turn around and say anything, she was on her knees taking all of me in her mouth.

"Fuck, I'm about to cum already." I guided her head up and down even though she didn't need any help.

"Cum, in my mouth Rory. I missed tasting you." She stared into my eyes, as she handled me and had one of her hands playing in her pussy. I couldn't hold out any longer and released a big load down her throat. I pulled her pants down and laid her right there on the rug. I devoured her pussy like it was cake batter, and I was licking the bowl.

"Rory, make me cum. Suck that shit. Oh God. Just like that." I made her cum so many times she didn't want to move afterwards. My dick was standing at attention, and her pussy was wide open. I rammed him inside and she jumped. I wanted her pussy to be sore for weeks so she couldn't fuck anyone else.

"Rory, what are you doing? Shit. Don't stop." He was digging her nails in my arm.

"Cady, whose pussy is this?"

"It's yours baby." She moaned as her eyes rolled.

"Say it again."

"Rory, it's yours, I swear. Fuck, right there."

"Shitttttt, Cady. I'm cumming." I came so hard, I just laid there on top of her. We were so lost in one another, neither one of us heard the door open.

"You two motherfuckers just couldn't get enough of each other at the restaurant, huh?" Miles asked, stepping over us. I was still on top of Cady so he couldn't see her body. He kept his back turned so she could get dressed but still continued to talk shit.

"No, we couldn't. Is there a problem?" Cady asked him, and he shook his head laughing.

"Nah. But if that's what y'all going to do, I'm going to need you to put Chanel on the same page. I miss the fuck out of her, and I didn't even get caught with my pants down like this nigga did."

"Fuck you, Miles. Don't bring me into yo shit. You got a crazy ass ex fucking up cars and shit."

"I'm going upstairs, baby." Cady said.

"You staying the night."

"Oh, I can't?"

"You don't even have to ask." She walked up to me and grabbed my dick.

"Hurry up, and get rid of him. I need some more of this." She whispered in my ear before she left.

"You don't have to say it. I heard her. I'm out my nigga. Remember what I said. Get rid of Taylor if you wanna be happy with her."

“I know. I’m working on it, but you know how she is.”

“Don’t forget what I said, Cady.” He yelled up the stairs.

“She said come over now if you’re coming. Otherwise, she’ll see you another time.”

“Word. I’m out, bro. She don’t have to tell me twice.” He walked to the door.

“You stupid as hell.”

“Try not to get her pregnant, Rory. I don’t see any wrappers anywhere, and I know you didn’t use one earlier with y’all nasty asses.”

“Too late. I’m sure she already is.” He laughed, and I dapped him up. I locked the door and put the chain on it. I wasn’t worried about Taylor coming, because I changed all the locks to my house yesterday. I already made plans to cut her loose. I ran my ass upstairs to finish what we started.

Miles

I was shocked when Cadence told me Chanel said I could come over. I wasn't expecting it, and now I'm sitting outside her house smoking a blunt. I don't know why I'm acting like a high school kid about to go in some chicks' house for the first time. I felt my phone vibrate, and when I looked down, it was a text.

Chanel: *I'm about to lie down. You can sit in that car all night if you want. I'm not leaving my door unlocked, so once I'm sleep, that's it.*

I shook my head laughing, because it meant she was waiting and saw me sitting out here. I put the blunt out and went inside.

"It's about time. Why you acting like you scared or something?"

"Ain't nobody scared of you. I was smoking."

"Yea, ok. You could've smoked up here. Anyway, what did you want to talk about?" She closed the door and locked it. She had on some pajama pants with a tank top on and some damn bunny slippers. I didn't even know women wore them.

"Why you been ignoring me?"

"Look Miles, I like you a lot, but I'm not trying to get caught up with Tory. She is the reason my ex and I aren't together, and I'm not trying to be with you and repeat the cycle."

"What you mean she's the reason?" She explained to me how her ex was cheating on her with Tory and how they fought.

"Chanel, I'm not going to front, I'm feeling the hell out of you, and I wanna make you my girl. Did I go back to fucking Tory when you stopped speaking to me? Yes. Do I want her? No."

"So why keep screwing her if you don't want her!" She folded her arm across her chest.

"Because she lets me. I know it sounds crazy, but it is what it is." I shrugged.

"So why you chasing me if that's the case?"

"I just told you. I want you, and I want you for more than just sex." I wrapped my arms around her waist.

"Ok, so now what?"

"You tell me. Do you think you can rock with a nigga and be his girl or what?" She gave me this dumbass smirk.

"Yea, I guess. But you better keep that bitch away from me. I don't have time for her shit. She can't be coming up to my job either. I swear, I'm going to whoop her ass Miles." I pulled my phone out and called her ass again.

"Before I call her, I'm going to tell you I slept with her a couple of days ago." She shrugged her shoulders, as if she didn't care, but I knew she was upset about it. Tory thought I was coming over so I knew she would answer right away.

"Hey baby. Where are you?" She grinned, shaking her head.

"Tory, I'm calling to tell you, I'm not fucking with you like that anymore. I made Chanel my girl."

"WHAT? Really Miles? Does she know we fucked the other day?"

"Yup. I told her everything."

"Miles, why are you doing this to me?" She pretended to be upset.

"Tory, stop acting like you're hurt. You could care less who I'm with. You just don't want me with her."

"Why don't you come over and let me change your mind?" She attempted to talk sexy in the phone and it didn't work this time.

"Nah, I'm good."

"You said that the last time."

"Yea, but you fucked that up being childish. Oh, one other thing." Chanel sat on the couch.

"What?"

"I better not find out you been up to her job, fucked with her car, or said two words to her, or I'm fucking you up. Do you hear me?" When she didn't answer, I yelled making Chanel jump.

"DO YOU HEAR ME TORY?"

"Yea, Miles. Damn! Is that all you called me for?" How the hell she aggravated?

"Yup. Peace." I hung up on her and put my phone on the table.

"Chanel, I'm serious about you." I went to say something else, but she was straddling me with her mouth covering mines.

"Damn baby, did you miss me?"

"You know I did." She removed her tank top.

"All you had to do was call my number."

"Shut up and fuck me. I need to feel you inside me right now." She unbuckled my jeans and hopped on my dick. We both let out a soft moan, as she clenched her pussy muscles on it.

"I missed you, Chanel. Fuck, this feels so good." She bounced down harder and faster. Her moans were driving me insane, and I couldn't hold out any longer.

"Shit, I'm cumming, baby girl." She jumped off and took him in her mouth sucking all my babies out.

"Mmmmm, Miles you taste good." I carried her in the bedroom and tied her hands up to the bedpost. I found something to do the same with her legs.

"Miles, what are you doing?" I licked my lips and dove in headfirst. I stuck my finger in her ass and sucked on her clit. Her river flowed rapidly in between her legs. I kept going and watched her have multiple orgasms.

"Oh shit, Miles. I can't take any more." I stood up and untied her feet only. I climbed in between, and put her legs on my shoulder. I entered her slowly and then sped up. She couldn't grab onto me, and it was driving her crazy.

"Miles, please, I can't take anymore." I was getting ready to stop when her leg started shaking. I wanted to cum with her, so I went faster and felt my nut building.

"I'm about to cum with you baby." I told her, as I watched a few tears coming down her face. I guess the shit was so good it made her cry.

"Miles, Oh Myyyyyyy Godddddddd. I love you. Shitttttt! Here I cummmmm…." She shouted.

"Let it go baby. I'm with you." We exploded at the same time. Fuck, I hope I didn't get her pregnant. I am not ready for any damn kids.

"Come on, Chanel."

"What Miles?" I untied her and she rolled over.

"I know you like to take a shower afterwards."

"I can't move Miles. Please, I just want to sleep."

"Yea, I wore that ass out." I went to take a shower, and when I came out, she was passed out. I put some water and soap on one a rag, cleaned her up, then laid in the bed with her. She snuggled up underneath me, as I lay there with my hand behind my head. I could get used to this.

Cadence

Rory and I have been fucking like rabbits for the past few weeks. I know it was stupid of me to make that bet with Taylor, but I needed to know if he was serious about ending it with her. I can't even be mad, because legally, that's his wife, and I'm the side chic. Am I ok with that? Hell no; but the love I have for him won't allow me to walk away.

I pulled up at Chili's to meet Rick for a lunch date. He was the guy Rory saw me at the restaurant with not too long ago. He was tall, dark, and handsome. He had a bald head and light brown eyes. The way his body was made, showed he stayed in the gym. We have been dating for about a month now, but I was still sleeping with Rory. He didn't have to know, because Rick and I wernet sexualy active with ine another.

"Hey beautiful." He kissed my cheek, as I went to sit down.

"Well, don't you look good today?" He was the perfect man for me, but I couldn't get past my love for Rory.

After we ate, he invited me to his house for a nightcap. I didn't mind. Shit, Rory had a wife. I parked my car behind his and went in behind him. He lived in a two-bedroom condo and you can tell it was a bachelor pad.

"Do you want something to drink?" He asked, grabbing water for himself. I shook my head no. He sat next to me and turned the radio on.

The quiet storm was on 107.5 WBLS. I may be young, but the songs from the 80's and 90's were on point. We started talking about our goals and dreams when he leaned in for a kiss. At first, I was hesitant, but once he slid his tongue inside, he had me.

He kneeled down in front of me and took my shoes off to massage my feet. I'll admit, he had me in heaven the way he was working on my feet. He took my socks off, stuck my toes in his mouth and sucked on them one-by-one. I could feel tingling in between my legs.

He unbuckled my jeans, and instead of stopping him, I lifted up a little to help him get them and my panties off. Call me what you want, but I wanted this. He spread my legs as wide as they could go and smiled.

"Cadence, you have one of the most prettiest pussy's I've ever seen." I covered my face with my hands. I still had to get used to a man complimenting me.

They always say it takes a second to tear someone down, but it takes forever to build them back up. Tristan had scarred me so bad, I couldn't tell when a man was being honest.

He pulled my body closer to the edge of the couch and let his tongue go up and down the lips. My body shuttered at the first touch.

He stuck his tongue inside my hole and sucked on my pearl. He was slurping and sucking at the same time. I was trying my hardest to hold in my orgasm, but it was no use. He pulled it out of me in minutes, and I loved all of it. He and Rory were in a race for first place when it came to eating pussy.

"Damn girl, that pussy taste good as hell." He said and made me cum all over his face again. He lifted my shirt up and unsnapped my bra, causing my breast to come out. He made love to both of them until he was satisfied. He threw his tongue in my mouth and kissed me with so much passion, I was about to bust off the kiss alone. His hands found their way in between my legs. The way I grinded on his hands gave me pleasure, but I wanted to feel him inside me.

He stood up and grabbed my hand to follow him in one of the bedrooms. There was a king-sized bed with black satin sheets and a comforter to match. I didn't even care what the rest of the room looked like. I climbed in the bed on all fours to get comfortable, but he stopped me in that exact position. His tongue found my ass and his fingers were massaging my clit. I was in heaven, and there was no coming down off the cloud he had me on.

"Damn, Rick. I'm about to cum again." I let loose, and he sucked all of it up. I rolled over on my back and watched him get a condom out the nightstand. I peeked to see what he was working with, and I was satisfied. He wasn't as big as Rory, but definitely bigger than Tristan. He took his time entering me. The way his dick filled me up, felt like it was a perfect match.

"Oh shit, Cadence. This pussy not only taste good, but it feels good. Don't take this from me." I didn't know what he meant by that, so I didn't respond. My legs were over his shoulder as he pounded away. I wanted to see if Rory was telling the truth about my riding skills so I told him I wanted to change positions. I guided myself down slowly and rocked back and forth.

"Shit Cadence. You about to make me wife you up with this pussy."

"How does it feel Rick?" He tried to grab on my hips, and I smacked his hands away. I went up and down squeezing his dick like Rory taught me.

"It feels so good I can't even explain it. Don't stop." I smirked, when his eyes was closed, and I gave him what he wanted. I bounced faster and faster, and then went in circles. I leaned back touching his legs and went up and down. He looked down as his dick go in and out, and I swear I heard him say my name.

"Cadence." I heard him say softly. Yes, I was riding the shit out of his dick.

"Fuck Rick. I'm getting ready to cum." He sat up kissing my chest and circling my clit.

"Get it, baby. Let it go Cadence."

"Shit. Oh shit, Rick. Here I cummmm. Oh God. That was so good. Shit." I was literally out of breath.

"Turn over Cadence." I knew he hadn't cum yet. I turned around, and he entered me with so much force, I had to jump forward a little bit.

"Shit, Cadence. You better not give my pussy away. This is mine now." *Why the fuck does everybody keep saying that? This is my pussy.*

"Rick, don't stop. Cum with me baby." He pumped faster and harder, and we both finished at the same time.

He went in the bathroom to take the condom off and got back in the bed with me. He pulled me closer to him, and we both fell asleep naked.

The next day, I woke up around ten to my phone going off. I felt Rick's arms still wrapped around me, as I reached for it. It was Rory. I didn't know if I should answer it, so I hit ignore. Even though I wasn't his girl, I still felt like shit for sleeping with Rick; but fuck it, I enjoyed it. I went to get out the bed, and Rick pulled me back in. He kissed me with morning breath and all.

"I want some more before you go." I was about to say something, but he went under the covers. We ended up sexing each other up until afternoon.

****

I parked in my driveway and saw Chanel's car there. I took my stuff out and did the walk of shame to my front door. She and my mom were in the kitchen drinking coffee.

"Ok. Spill it bitch. Rory has been calling asking where you were, so don't come in here saying you were with him." Chanel knew me like a book.

"Let me take a shower and change clothes, and I'll come back to tell you." I let the hot water beat down on my skin and washed my body. I threw on some stretch pants and a t-shirt. Chanel and my mom were sitting in the living room watching TV.

"Ok. What's up?" I sat in the loveseat with my feet underneath me. I told them how Rick and I went to Chili's, but went back to his house and had sex all night and again this morning. They were both cheesing like Cheshire cats.

"What? Why are you smiling like that?" Chanel put her coffee cup on a coaster and came to sit by me.

"I'm happy for you, Cady."

"I feel bad though, because I love Rory."

"Girl, bye. I don't care how many times you sleep with him or how many times he tell you he's leaving Taylor, he's still married and you're the mistress. It's about time you start worrying about Cady and no one else."

"She's right, Cady. Don't feel bad for venturing out. You are a single woman doing single things." The doorbell rang as my mom spoke. She went to answer it, and I knew who it was before he entered the room.

"Cady, can I talk to you?" I could tell he was mad, but I had to take care of me. My mom and Chanel went upstairs while we talked. He sat across from me with his arms on his legs.

"Cady, I'm going to ask you this one time." I looked at him like he was crazy.

"What is it Rory?" He stared in the air and blew his breath out.

"Where were you last night and this morning?"

"Do you really want me to answer? You know the saying is don't ask a question you don't really want the answer to."

"I wouldn't ask you if I didn't wanna know."

"I stayed the night with a friend." I saw the look on his face and knew I hurt him. I just didn't understand why.

"Did you sleep with him?" He stared in my eyes, and I felt like shit, but I answered him.

"Not that it's any of your business, but yes I did."

"Ok." He stood up.

"Ok. That's it?"

"What do you want me to say Cady?" He shrugged.

"I don't know… something more than that."

"Cady, you are a grown woman. What? Do you want me to get upset and start degrading you or putting my hands on you? Is that what you want?"

"No, but."

"But what Cady? Do you want to know if I'm hurt? Yes. I'm hurt like a motherfucker. The damage is done, and there's nothing I can do."

"You're right, you can't. How dare you come over here questioning me about who I'm sleeping with when you're still married?" He didn't say shit. He shook his head, laughing, and it was pissing me off.

"You have me sitting around being your mistress/side chick, and you think I'm supposed to be ok with that. Rory, I loved you with all my heart, and you hurt me over and over. I deserve to be happy."

"Cady, I agree with you a hundred percent. You deserve to be happy, and even though I was married to Taylor, I explained my situation to you. I messed up and fucked her a couple of times, but I swear, after the night we slept together this last time, I haven't been with her." I was really feeling like shit, but I was standing my ground with him; he was still wrong.

"I'm supposed to believe that. I mean, I did before, and look where it got me." I started walking behind him yelling. He stood at the door and turned around, took both of my hands in his and interlocked our fingers together.

"Cady, do you know why I was calling you all day yesterday?"

"No." I removed my hands from him and folded up my arms.

"I wanted to tell you the judge granted my divorce from Taylor under the no-fault divorce. He told me that because she kept fighting it, he wanted to know why. When we got to court, I had pictures of her with Deshawn, which is adultery. She even tried to get some money out of me, but my father had an airtight prenup when we were married, so she got nothing. I was so happy she was outta my life, and I could start over with you and celebrate, but you didn't answer." He moved closer to me.

"I know I hurt you Cady, but I told you I needed to tie up loose ends, and you were ok with it."

"That's just it, Rory. I was never ok with being a mistress."

"Then, you should've told me when I laid everything out for you." He looked me up and down woth a disgusting look; maimg me uncomfortable.

"Listen, I'm not going to keep you any longer. I just wanted to make sure you were ok, because your best friend didn't even know where you were, and that's not like you. I hope you're happy, and I won't bother you anymore." He kissed my cheek and left.

I slammed the door and ran upstairs to my room. All I could do was cry, but I didn't know if I was crying because I was in love with him, or because I knew this was it.

<u>Tristan</u>

I was calling my boy all night and this morning to see what happened last night. I sat in my uncle's crib pissed off that I even allowed him to talk me into going along with this plan. I knew Rory wanted to kill me, but I didn't want Cadence hurt in the process.

I treated her like shit, but she stayed loyal and what did I do? I tried to kill her boyfriend, because she finally got tired of my shit. I threw back another shot, as I waited for my boy to come by.

"Looks like your boy handled his business last night, into this morning." My uncle Mace walked in with his two goons by his side.

"What are you talking about?" He went to the TV and popped a disc in. He hit the input button, and the sight on the screen had me fuming.

"Yo, turn that shit off."

"No, nephew. I want you to see this." He turned the volume up so I could hear it better. The more I listened, the more hurt I was. To see this shit, was going to kill Cady's family reputation and her.

"This video will hit the internet within minutes unless we can reach a deal. Shit, I should send this to Vivid Entertainment and see if I could make some money."

"This wasn't part of the plan. When and why were there cameras in the house?" I saw my boy walk in with a grin on his face. He dapped everyone up and sat down on the couch.

"You were in on this shit?" I asked standing face-to-face with him. He smirked before he answered.

"I'm the one who suggested it." I punched his ass in the face. My uncle stepped in the middle before anything else could happen.

"Listen, Tristan. You are lucky someone stepped in to help you out, because none of these niggas wanted to have anything to do with you. This is our leverage to get the bounty off your head. What you need to be doing is thanking his ass for it?"

"Thank him. You think I'm going to thank him for this shit." I went in the room and slammed the door. I was mad, I got myself caught up in this bullshit. I laid on the bed and thought about where my life was going at this point.

"Get up, yo." One of my uncle's goons came in.

"For what?" They were really starting to irk my nerves.

"Your uncle just got off the phone with Donovan. We are about to go over there, and he wanted to know if you were riding.

"Nah, I'm good. I don't wanna be there when you show him." He walked out, and my uncle came in.

"Look, I know how you're feeling, but this was the only way."

"Yea, but it's a fucked up way to go about it."

"In this game, no one plays fair. Trust me when I say, I'm sure the bounty will be removed before I come back." He dapped me up and left.

<u>*Rory*</u>

I left Cady's house a few days ago, and I admit when she told me she slept with someone else, it fucked me up. I didn't want to believe my boy when he told me she was at Chili's, and he followed her back to some dude's place. I had to hear it from the horse's mouth. The way she said it made me feel like she didn't care about a nigga no more. I took it for what it was an d left her alone.

I was sitting in my office at the gym when Donovan called to say, I needed to find Miles and get to his house quick. I ran out of there thinking something was wrong with Cadence.

I pulled up and noticed those same Yukon's from before, made sure my piece was in my waist and stepped out. Miles parked and asked me the same question we were both about to ask Donovan.

We stepped in, and the nigga Mace had a smug look on his face. You know, the look like he had something that was going to piss me off. We wet down the hall and his team were all sitting in the living room having a stare down.

"Now that you're here, we can get this party started." Mace said, making my blood boil. I hated this man, and I didn't even know why Donovan would conduct a sit down in his house with him.

"What's all this about Mace?" I heard Donovan ask.

"I think we've come up with a resolution to take the bounty off my nephew's head." I shook my head laughing, because he was still trying.

"Oh, yea. And what's that?"

"Donovan, may I?" He asked, holding up a disk. D gave him a head nod, and he put it on. The goons he was with had a smirk on their face. Two of the guys looked familiar, but I couldn't place them.

We sat back waiting for the video to play, when I noticed Cady sitting on a couch talking to the guy in the room.

"What the fuck is this?" Donovan slammed his drink on the table.

"This right here is going to keep that bounty off my nephew's head." The video kept playing when Mace hit fast forward. Dude was kissing Cady, and she didn't stop him. He fast-forward a little more, and this nigga was in between her legs.

"Turn it off."

"Wait, it gets better. He fast-forwarded it some more, and Cady was on top riding his dick and moaning.

"Turn it the fuck off before I blow your fucking head off." I had my gun against his temple so fast his boys didn't have time to react. They all had guns against their heads as well. D snatched the remote out his hands and shut the video off. He took the disc out and broke it in half.

"It doesn't matter. I have a few copies, and if that bounty isn't taken off my nephew's head, it will hit the Internet in the next hour." He stood with his hands up. I didn't want to do it, but I thought about Cady and how this would kill her. I looked at D and Miles, and they both nodded their heads in agreement. My finger was itching to pull the trigger, but what if there were multiple videos. It would defeat the purpose, because it would get out anyway.

"Where are the rest of the videos?" He pulled out two more.

"Is that it?" Miles asked him.

"Now, why would I give you the only leverage I have? The one I have is in a safe place for collateral. If anything happens to my nephew on account of *The Bloods*, this video will be released."

"Get the fuck out of here." I heard D yell. They walked out like they won the battle, but little did they know, the war hasn't even started.

I waited for them to leave and took off to Cady's house. So many thought were running through my mind, I barely had my car in park before I jumped out. I started banging on the door. She opened it wearing just a t-shirt and slippers.

"What is it, Rory?" She had the nerve to act as if she had an attitude. She shut the door and locked it.

"Come here." I grabbed her hand and walked up to her bedroom with her. I put the DVD but didn't hit play.

"Cady, how well did you know the guy you've been seeing?"

"Why?" She had an attitude.

"Just answer the question."

"I don't have to tell you shit." She was pissing me the fuck off.

"Cady, just answer the question."

"I have been seeing him for about a month. He told me he worked as a mechanic. Are you going to tell me what this is about?"

"Was that the first time you slept with him?" That question was more or less for my own conscience. I was sleeping with her at the same time.

"Yes, Rory. What is this about?"

"Cady. I'm about to show you something that's probably going to make you mad. I need you to know it's being handled." I pushed the DVD in and let her watch.

"Where did you get this from?" I didn't answer. When he pulled her pants down, she covered her mouth. She fast forwarded the entire video and cried.

"Who did this?" I saw the tears falling down her face.

"Tristan and his uncle set it up. They're using this as leverage for me not to kill him. If I do, this will go on the Internet." She plopped down on the bed next to me. I wanted to hold her and tell her everything would be ok, but I was still mad she gave herself to someone else so I didn't. I took the DVD out and broke it in half.

"Rory?"

"Yea."

"I'm sorry. I didn't mean to hurt you." I sat in the chair staring at her, as she balled up in a fetal position on the bed. I didn't know what to say so I just stayed there until she went to sleep. I pulled the covers over her and shut the light off.

"Rory, please don't leave." I heard her whisper.

"Cady, I don't want to, but I think its best."

"Rory, please. I need you." I sat back in the chair. She lifted the covers up and scooted back motioning for me to get in with her.

"Cady, that's not a good idea." She put the covers down and rolled on her back.

"Rory, I'm pregnant."

"What did you just say?" She grabbed something white off her nightstand and handed it to me. There were two pink lines staring me in my face. Inside I was smiling, because I did what I set out to do.

"What do you want to do about it Cady?" I asked to see where her head was.

"What do you want to do?" She threw it back at me.

"I'll support whatever decision you make."

"I'm keeping it. We can co-parent." I was shocked when she said that. I lifted the covers and got in bed with her.

"I know I hurt you Rory, but I am still in love with you, and I want you to be in me and the baby's life. I understand if you decide to just be around the baby." She had her head on my chest.

"Cady, I'm still in love with you, too, and I hurt you as well. We both fucked up, and the only thing we can do is move past it if we want a future, if that's what you want."

"I do, Rory."

"I love you Cadence. Are you done with dude?" She nodded her head yes and deleted his information out her phone. She slid her hands down my pants, but I stopped her.

"Nah. We starting over fresh, and there's no way I'm fucking you when we first meet. Plus, you had sex with dude a few days ago; we waiting at least two weeks." She poked her lips out. I kissed them, and she fell asleep in my arms while I laid there figuring out how I was about to kill all them motherfuckers.

Donovan

After Mace displayed that video of my niece in front of everyone, I wanted to kill his ass on the spot, but I had to keep my cool. He knew the rules of the game, so him pulling this was a bitch move. I can't even imagine how many times they may have watched it, and knowing he had more, made me livid. I called my sister and brother-in-law, Marlon, over to let them know what was going on. My sister and her husband rushed inside my office.

"Is everything ok?" My sister asked. I explained to them what Mace did, and I think Marlon was ready to go find him.

"Cady told us." Marlon said.

"How is Cady taking it?" I asked them.

"I spoke to Rory and he said she was ok. The night he told her, she cried most of the night. She has been staying with him at his house since."

We sat in my office discussing the plans I had when Cady and Rory walked in hand in hand.

"I'm glad you guys are all here. I need to tell you something." I could see how nervous she was. Rory took a seat, and she sat on his lap.

"What's wrong?" I asked her.

"As you all know, Rory and I have been together off and on for almost a year now."nShe was fidgeting with her hands.

"Ok." Marlon said.

"I just wanted to be the first to tell you, he and I just came from the doctors, and I'm four weeks pregnant." My sister jumped up, hugged her, and asked to see the sonogram photo. Marlon and I just sat there staring at him.

"Cady, you and your mom go in the kitchen so we can talk to Rory?" She was skeptical to leave but she stepped out.

"Congratulations, Rory. Did you tell your parents yet?" I asked.

"Yea. We stopped by there first. My mom is excited."

"Are you sure that's your baby?" Marlon asked looking at him.

"Yea, that's my baby. She only slept with the other dude once. Even if the baby wasn't mines, I would still be there for her."

"Do you love Cadence?" Marlon was throwing questions back to back at him for some reason.

"Yes. I'm in love with Cady, and I don't see myself with anyone else." Rory sat up in the chair where before he as slouched down.

"With all due respect; I know when she and I met, I had a situation, but it was something I did when I was young and dumb. I did everything I could to rid myself of my ex, and now that it's done, I can put all my focus on Cady." We both shook our heads. I stood up to give him a hug and Marlon followed suit.

"Rory, I want you and Cady to keep this quiet for now until we find out what Mace and his crew are up to. I know we called a truce for now, but you and I both know it's just a matter of time before you get at him." He just grinned and stood up to leave.

"D?"

"What up, Rory?"

"You know he fucked up when he hurt Cady?"

"I know. But now he has to deal with what's going to happen to him." He shut the door behind him. Marlon and I stepped out and heard arguing going on. It was Cady and my sister.

"How dare you ask me if it's ok that no one get at Tristan?"

"I'm just saying, his mom was very upset, and I would feel the same way if someone was trying to kill you."

"Really. Would you be ok with giving him a pass if I died?" My sister turned her face up when she said that.

"That's what I thought. Rory, can we please go?" She grabbed his hand and headed towards the front door.

"Rory, can you please think about it?" She yelled out. He walked back up to my sister.

"Cady is safe with me but I want you to think about something." He glancd over at Cady and then back at my soster.

"The beef was between him and I until he shot her. Now, I understand you're a mom, and his mom made you feel bad, but if Cady killed or shot at him, you can bet she would try and have her killed immediately. You wouldn't have even been able to step foot on her property to ask the same thing she did." Rory turned around and left.

I told my sister, Cady would be mad when her mother asked her that dumb shit. Oh well; she needed to hear it from her.

Cadence

I was still in shock when I left my uncle's after hearing my mom asking if I wanted to spare Tristan's life. I mean, whether he was aiming for Rory or not, he should've never had a gun on him anyway. The crazy part is, I didn't even think Tristan cared about me enough to do some shit like that. Now, his mom and uncle are begging for his life, yet they taped me having sex with someone from their crew. Watching myself on the video showed me no one could be trusted.

When Rory came by the day after to tell me his divorce was final, I felt like shit. He kept telling me to wait for him, and me being spiteful, went out and jumped on the next available dick. Don't get me wrong, Rick's dick game was good, and so was the head. It just wasn't enough to steal my heart from Rory.

Since he was ok making a video of me without my knowledge, he fucked up any chance he may have had if Rory and I didn't work out.

"Hey baby. Are you ok?" Rory asked, sitting next to me. He put my legs on his and rubbed the back of my calves.

"Yea. I just don't understand why all of this keeps happening to me."

"Don't worry; I got you." He pecked my lips.

"Can I ask you something, Rory?"

"Go ahead baby."

"I want you to be honest with me."

"Ok."

"Do you think you will cheat on me?" He stopped rubbing my legs.

"Why would you ask me some dumb shit like that?"

"I'm asking, because you were cheating on your wife with me."

"Cady, what Taylor and I had was more of an agreement than a marriage. Yes, in the eyes of the law, we were married. I did that when I was young and dumb so she couldn't testify against me if it came down to it. I know I fucked up by sleeping with her when I knew you had feelings for me, but you and I never made it official."

"It doesn't make it right, Rory."

"I know it doesn't. Once I slept with you, I should've stopped with her and I'm sorry. The night you were supposed to come over, Taylor text me and got there before you. We were discussing working on our marriage, and I kept telling her no. Unfortunately, I had been drinking and smoking before she got there. She started waking my man up and dropped to her knees. I should've stopped it, but I didn't. I never thought about you walking in, because you didn't have a key. Matter of fact, how did you get in?" I started telling him what Taylor said at the bar, and how she made a bet she could sleep with him.

"How could you do that Cadence?" He pushed my legs off his lap.

"What? I wanted to know if you were serious about you and I."

"So you send my ex over to seduce me?" He stood up and began pacing the living room floor.

"Here I am feeling fucked up about it, and you and her set the shit up. What the fuck? You may as well have recorded it."

"Rory, it's not that serious."

"What you mean it's not that serious? Would you like it if I told you, I sent that motherfucker to see if he could fuck you?" I looked at him like he was crazy.

"I would never do something like that so fix your face." He plopped down on the couch and blew his breath out. I tried to straddle him, but he moved me off if him. I didn't know why he was that mad; he was the one who slept around.

I sent a text to Chanel for her to come pick me up. I needed to get out of here. I stood to go upstairs to get ready when the doorbell rang.

"What do you want Taylor?" I asked when I opened the door.

"Is Rory here?" She had a smirk on her face.

"What the fuck you want Taylor?" I stood there waiting for her to answer.

"Good. Both of you are here and can hear my surprise."

"What are you talking about? Taylor, I don't nobody have time for yo shit." She was pissing him off even more. Maybe he couldn't stand her.

"I just wanted to inform you and this chick that, even though we're divorced now, your child will be here in eight months."

"What baby?" I asked with my arms folded.

"Oh, Cadence remember when we made that bet at the bar." She tried to shout me out. I'm glad I did mention it.

"He already knows about it Taylor."

"Well anyway, we went at it for a while and guess what? Neither one of us thought about wearing a condom, so BAM! You can have him now, but just know, we will be seeing a lot of each other."

"Yea, ok." Rory stood there in shock.

"Don't worry. When the baby is born, you can take all the test you want and the baby will still be yours." I went to close the door in her face, but he stopped me.

"Are you sure it's my baby Taylor?" Now, I was the one in shock to hear, he was entertaining it.

"Yea, Rory. I just came back from the doctors." She handed him an ultrasound picture. I wanted to leave, but I refused to give her the satisfaction.

"Call me when it's time for the next appointment." She walked to her car with a smile on her face. He closed the door, and I could feel him burning a hole in mine.

"What?" I snapped.

"Don't what me, Cady. This is your fault."

"How the hell is this my fault? I didn't tell you to stick your dick in her."

"No you didn't. But you wanted to be childish and make a bet on my dick, and now look what happened."

"You knew it was her you were fucking; you could've said no."

"This all could've been avoided, and you're right, but I was sitting here waiting for you and getting drunk. I didn't expect it to happen, but it did. Now I'm going to be a father to a baby whose mother I can't stand all because of a stupid bet that the woman I'm in love with made being petty. I never wanted a baby mama. I wanted a wife, a family. Not have a baby outside of who I'm with. DAMMIT, CADENCE!" he was furious.

"What did you expect? You slept with her with no condom."

"That's just it Cady. I've never fucked her without one, because I knew I didn't want kids with her. You sent her over here, and I was so drunk, I slipped up. Now I'm stuck with her being in my life forever, when it took so much outta me to get rid of her. FUCK!!!! He grabbed his keys and stormed out the house. Chanel came in as he was leaving.

"What happened?" I told her what Taylor said.

"I told you the bet wasn't a good idea."

"Really, Chanel? Whose side are you on?"

"I'm not on anyone's side, but I see where he's coming from. Cady, he did everything to rid himself of her so he could be with you."

"I'm sure I wasn't the reason he did it."

"Cady listen to yourself. He may have been taking his time handling her, but once you and him started sleeping together, he did everything in his power to expedite it. That man loves you to death, despite your *"I don't give a fuck"* attitude."

"How is he going to be mad at me when he slept with her?"

"He's mad because you set the shit up. You sent her over here knowing her intentions. Yes, he slept with her, but didn't you say he was drunk?" I nodded my head.

"Ok, so we all know when someone is drunk, their sex drive entices. I'm not saying what he did was right, but she probably sucked him off or some shit to initiate it."

"Still he -" She cut me off.

"No, Cady. You don't get to put it all on him. If you never went along with Taylor and took your ass home to him, this wouldn't have happened."

"Fuck it. What's done is done. All I can do is be mad. I'm having my own baby, so if he wants to be with her, then he can." He stepped inside just as I said that.

"Is that what you think Cady? You think I wanna be with her now that she's pregnant?" I was still trying to be tough like it wasn't killing me inside.

"At this point Rory, I don't even care if you do or not anymore."

"You don't care?" I sucked my teeth and went to get my purse. He grabbed my arm and had me against the wall.

"You don't care, Cady?" I shook my head no.

"Get off of her Rory." Chanel was pulling his arm. He wasn't hitting me he; he just had his body pressed against mine, holding my wrist.

"Cady, tell me right now if this is what you want." He pointed back and forth from me to him.

"Tell me right now. If it's not, I will walk out of your life."

"I don't know, Rory. This is all too much for me right now." I felt myself about to cry.

"Too much for you? Are you serious? I'm the one whose about to have a baby by a spiteful woman, all because you were trying to prove a point. You know what, Cady? I think it's best you leave before I say something I'm not going to regret."

"Are you serious right now?"

"Yes. I am."

"So you're just going to make me leave over this?"I was leaving anyway but it was my choice.

"Cady, I'm done talking about it. Matter of fact, I don't

think you and I are going to work." I saw all the hurt in his face as he said it.

"Wait. You're breaking up with me?"

"Goodbye, Cady." Chanel looked at me shaking her head.

"Can you believe this shit?" I asked her with tears falling down my face. I started picking up my things.

"Just go. Anything you have here, I'll drop it off later." He had the door open waoting for me to leave.

"Rory, can we talk about this?"

"Nah. I'm good. This is my fault for sticking my dick in her, right? I don't want to see you or her anytime soon. I'm done with both of you."

"You're done with me?" I looked at him with my face still covered with tears.

"This is how you treat me now?"

"I will always love you Cady, but this shit you two did got my head fucked up. I could see if I was just some nigga you didn't care about. Shit, was the bet worth it? Did you get what you wanted?" I put my head down and walked out the door. I fucked up, and I know there was no way I could fix it. I had Chanel drop me off at my uncles' house instead. I was still pissed at my mom, and this was the safest place for me.

"Hey Cady. You ok?" My uncle asked. He was watching TV in the living room. I laid my head on his lap and told him what happened.

"That was foul, Cady."

"You too, Uncle D."

"Cady, you're a grown ass woman. If you're looking for me to side with you because you're my niece, you can forget it. I love you to death, but what you did was wrong. Regardless if he did it, you pushed him, and you can't blame anyone but yourself. Rory is very stubborn, and once he says something, he doesn't go back on it."

"You think he's really done with me?"

"I don't know. All you can do is give him time to decide what he wants." We stayed up watching movies all nightband I sent Rory a message before I went to sleep.

Me: *I'm so sorry, Rory. I never meant to hurt you. I*

didn't think it would result in you sleeping with

her or having a baby. I wasn't thinking. I love you, and I hope I

haven't lost you for good. I put my phone down. The phone

vibrated letting me know I had a message. It was from him, but

I was scared to open it.

Rory: *Too late for regrets now. I'm stuck in a no-win*

situation with her. She's about to make my

life a living hell. I want to thank you for placing her back on

my life to do just that. I tried to love you Cady; even under the

circumstances, but that nigga scarred you so bad, you're doing

the same thing to me. I wish you nothing but the best.

He left the icon with the peace sign at the bottom of the

text. Damn, I guess I lost him for good this time. Oh well; it

will be my baby and me. He can have his life with her.

I jumped in the shower and laid there thinking of how I

fucked up. My next step is moving to start over. I just have to

figure out where.

Taylor

"I'm tired of this bitch already." I said out loud, as if I had an audience.

I went by Rory's house to tell him I was pregnant, and Cadence was there. I thought me and her an agreement that when she caught me fucking him, it was a wrap. What pissed me off the most is, he fucked her in the bathroom on my damn birthday thinking I didn't know.

She came out and waved, and he had some white shit in top of his pants. I didn't want to cause a scene, so I didn't say anything because he was still coming home with me. I thought he was anyway, until he dropped me off and left. I rode by his house later and saw her car parked there. That's when I knew it was time to get my man back.

The look on the bitch face was priceless when I told her. When Rory said he wanted to attend the next appointment, I'm not going to tell him until after. I didn't want him in any doctor's appointments with me. He didn't deserve to be after the shit he pulled.

I was meeting up with Tory for lunch to discuss Cadence's friend. She and Miles have been inseparable the last two months, and she was feeling some kind of way.

"Hey, Taylor. I'm glad you could meet me." She gave me a hug and sat back down.

"What's up?" I gave the waitress my drink order and sent her on her way. We were at one of the guys' restaurants, and I couldn't stand the help.

"I was thinking that you can help me come up with a plan for me to get Miles back." This chick was bugging.

"Why do you want him back? I thought you were fucking someone else."

"I don't want him back. I just don't want her to have him." She burst out laughing. I joined in, because I felt kind of the same way about Rory and Cadence, but the only difference is, I wanted him.

"What is it that you're trying to do? I mean, he's with her all the time. How do you think you're going to get in between?"

"I know where the bitch work and live." I shook my head.

"First, I'm going to get her dumb ass fired. I'll figure out what I'm going to do after that, but hey, that's a start." She laughed.

"Girl, you are crazy. I could see if you wanted him back."

"Fuck that. Miles was my cash cow, and now he won't give me a dime because of her." She was reallymad over him not giving her money. After the years they spent together, one would think she wanted him backf or love.

"Aren't you messing with someone who has money?"

"Yea, but ever since Rory and Miles took over those businesses, their money has quadrupled. Girl, he was taking me on shopping sprees and allowing me to buy shit that only celebrities get. Not to mention, he has a big ass dick." I let her vent until it was time to go. She really had no ambition to do shit but mess up Mile's relationship. *What the hell am I talking about? I'm getting ready to do the same thing.*

I hopped in my car and started driving when my phone started vibrating. I looked down, and it was Rory.

"What's up, Rory?"

"Can you stop by?" I was shocked that he invited me over, but who was I to turn down his invitation.

Rory

I called Taylor over to see if she was planning on keeping the baby for real and what her expectations were of me. I hate that her and Cady decided to play some dumb ass game to prove a point. Now, here I am with two baby mamas and no wife. The day Taylor came over, she sent a text asking to talk about the marriage.

"Rory, can I come over so we can discuss this marriage stuff?" I didn't think anything of it, so I told her yes. I knew Cady was coming, so she wouldn't be staying long anyway. She came inside, and I offered her a drink. We smoked two blunts, and the shots I was taking didn't make it any better.

"What you want to talk about?" She started going on and on about how we should make it work and not let someone else come in and tear us apart.

"Taylor, Cadence didn't tear us apart; you did."

"How, Rory?"

"When you fucked my boy. I'm not going to get over that. If I stay married to you, I will regret it." I looked at her.

"Taylor, there's someone out there for you and it's not me." She started crying, and I thought I was being the good guy by handing her a tissue. She took the tissue and reached over placing her lips on mine.

"Taylor, what are you doing?" I pushed her back. She lifted her shirt up and unsnapped her bra. Her titties were still as perky as I remember.

Taylor wasn't an ugly woman, so when she started stripping, my dick got hard. She was light-skinned with long hair. She had brown eyes, and a Coca-Cola body she flaunted every chance she got. Men would probably love to call her their woman but not me. I wanted her out of my life to build something with Cadence.

Anyway, she noticed my man standing at attention. I stood up before anything could happen, but she snatched my sweats and boxers down and put him in her mouth. The way she sucked me made me cum in no time.

I picked her up and carried her to my room. She threw me on the bed and rode my dick, until she came so hard, she collapsed on the bed. I was still erect, and instead of throwing her ass out, I turned her around and fucked her until I came.

"Shit, Taylor you have to go." I tossed her clothes at her while she laid there pulling the covers up. It was getting late, and I knew Cady would be on her way soon. It took Taylor almost a half hour before she decided to leave. I waited all night for Cady, and when she never showed, I started panicking.

I called Miles up, and he told me she was staying somewhere with Chanel. When I finallyn spoke to Cady, and she told me she saw Taylor and me fucking, I knew she was done.

I brought myself out of daydreaming when I heard the doorbell ringing. I opened the door, and Taylor was standing there looking sexy as hell. Even though I broke things off with Cady, I didn't want to fuck with Taylor like that either. I stepped aside so she could come in.

"Thanks for coming by Taylor."

"Anything for my baby daddy." I cringed when she said that. I hated to be associated with her as such.

"I wanna know what you think is gonna happen now that you told me you were pregnant?" She was taken aback by what I said.

"What do you mean?"

"I mean, I'm gonna take care of my kid, but I'm not taking care of you. If you thought being pregnant by me was going to make you rich, get those thoughts out of your mind."

"Nobody said that, but don't you think I should live comfortably with your baby?"

"Absolutely, but you still live at home, and don't pay any bills. Your parents don't want you to move out anyway. I'm not getting you an apartment just because, and I think any judge would agree with me."

"Oh, you think so?"

"I know so. See, he's going to ask why you would move out of a stable home to care for your kid. Then, he would make you get a job as well. Let alone, the fact we'd share custody, which I'm filing as soon as you have the baby, and it's confirmed that he or she is mine. Which means I will have the baby every other week, so child support will be denied." Her facial expression was priceless.

"Why are you doing me like this?"

"Taylor, you and Cady were being sneaky, and because of it, I now have two baby mommas. You know I've always told you I wanted a family with one woman having my kids."

"Wait. That bitch is pregnant too?" I saw the look of disgust on her face.

"Yes, she is. I don't think either one of you thought this little bet through. Y'all were so busy trying to get revenge on each other that now you're babies will be related." She rolled her eyes and sucked her teeth.

"My baby won't have a sibling unless it's by me." I snatched her stupid ass up by the collar.

"I better not ever hear you say no dumb shit like that. If that's my baby, you can guarantee they will be brought up together." I saw the fear in her face, as I dropped her back on the couch.

"Who are you? You never put your hands on me or even snatched me up."

"Fuck outta here with that shit Taylor. You playing these childish ass games with a kid who didn't ask to be here."

"Hmph. Let me guess. She's mad at you, so you're taking it out on me."

"Nah, we're not together anymore." I sat on the couch.

"Oh. Let me make you feel better then." She reached her hand in my pants, and I moved them.

"Not gonna happen. I may not be with her, but she still has my heart."

"Oh, you're in love with her?"

"Yes, I am." I helped her off the couch and led her to the door. She went to say something, and I shut it in her face. My next stop was to see Cady. She was at her uncle's, because she was still mad at her mom.

She opened the door with an attitude when I got there. I took her hand and went to the room she was staying at.

"How far along are you?"

"I went to the doctor's today, and unfortunately, I'm four weeks along." I ran my hand down my face. I had two baby moms having my kids around the same time. What the fuck was I thinking?"

"Ok. This is what's about to happen."

"Rory, don't tell me what's about to happen like I have no say so."

"Cadence, be quiet. This shit got me fucked up." I closed rthe bedroom door.

"Like I said; I'm putting you up in your own place; it will be furnished, and I will give you money to buy the baby whatever is needed. I'll stay at my place, but I need to make sure you two are ok."

"Rory, you don't have to do that."

"I know, but I want my baby born in his own house. I don't have a problem with you living at home, but I think we both know you wanna be on your own. All I ask is that, if you decide to deal with another guy, just don't have him at the house. If it gets serious, and you fall in love with him, then I will rent the place out, and you can find somewhere else to live."

"You're really done with me Rory?" I could see her eyes getting glassy.

"I don't know right now Cady. My heart is with you, but my mind is elsewhere. What you did was foul as hell, and if it wasn't you, I probably would've beat the shit out of you."

"You would put your hands on a woman?"

"No. I just said if it wasn't you. I did almost hit Taylor today for talking some dumb shit, but I caught myself."

"Wow."

"Look, she was talking reckless about the baby, so I snatched her ass up."

"Oh, ok. Well, when do you want to start apartment shopping? I'm ready to get out of here." She stood up, but I pulled her down on my lap.

"Cady, I love you so much, but what you did got me thinking that this isn't really what you want." I went to finish, but she put her finger to my mouth.

"I love you too Rory, and I'm so sorry I hurt you like that. Even though you slept with her, it was my fault for pushing her in your arms. Please don't leave me."

"Let's just get you your own place, and we'll figure out something later." She laid down in front of me and pulled me on top of her. I could've gotten up, but I didn't.

"Make love to me Rory." I put my tongue in her mouth and let it slow dance with her for a few minutes.

My hand slid up her shirt and rubbed both of her breasts gently. I took them in my mouth one at a time; sucking and licking. She had her hand on the back of my head. I took her pants down, and my mouth watered as soon as I looked at her bottom lips.

"Cady, I can't say enough how good your pussy is. It's killing me that you gave it to someone else." She pulled me back up and kissed me aggressively. I went back down and dove right into my favorite place on her body. My tongue went in and out of both holes making her scream out my name.

"Rory, I love you so much baby. I'm cumming." She had so many juices escaping her body, I wasn't able to catch all of it at first. I sucked her insides out until it felt like she was dry. She rolled me over and took me in her mouth.

"Damn, Cady." I grabbed the back of her hair and watched as she made her cheeks go in and out while she sucked. I came so hard, I didn't think I could move. She stroked him until he woke up again. She jumped on top and pounced on it.

"Oh, my God, Rory. I'm cumming. Oh shit…" She fell back. I made her toot that ass in the air. I fucked the shit out of Cady; taking all my anger out on her. She didn't complain one time, which let me know, she knew she deserved it.

"I'm about to cum, Cady."

"Go ahead, baby. I'm already pregnant." When she said that, it made me go harder.

"Shit, Cady. I got you pregnant on purpose." I yelled out as my nut started rising.

"No you didn't. I wanted a baby by you, so I let you cum inside me with no regret. Shit, I'm about to cum. Oh God; here it comes."

"Me, too. Ahhhh, fuck Cady. I love you, girl." We both laid there trying to catch our breath. I was still shocked she wanted me to get her pregnant.

"Why did you let me get you pregnant?" I asked, holding onto her.

"I love you Rory, and after I saw how hurt you were when I lost the baby, I wanted to give you what I knew you wanted the most."

"You are what I want." I told her.

"Does it really matter at this point? You were trying to be sneaky with it." I smiled, and she smacked me in the arm.

"Now what?" She asked, playing with the little bit of hair I had on my chest.

"I don't know. Let's take a shower and look online for apartments. I need to get my baby his own room." I bent down to kiss her stomach, but her pussy was calling me. Needless to say, we sexed each other a few more times before we got in the shower. Her legs were so weak, I had to help her up. I stayed a little while longer and went to see my boy.

Miles

Rory asked me and Chanel to ride with them to the store to scope out baby furniture. I'll admit, I didn't want any kids, but watching my boy get excited had me feeling like it was time. I mean, he had two kids on the way at the same time.

Cady had us in all types of furniture stores until she found what she wanted. Rory paid for all of it, but it wasn't to be delivered until she found a place. I thought it was bad luck to shop so early, but I guess the bad luck was when they lost the first one.

Chanel wanted to go to Macy's afterwards to get a few things, so Rory and I walked down to Foot Locker. The new Jordan's came out, and we both had someone hold our sizes. We got the girls a pair from kids' Foot Locker. Their feet were small in boys' sizes, so we didn't have to put them on hold because we knew their sizes would be there.

I heard some niggas talking and low and behold, when we turned around, we were face-to-face with Tristan, the Rick guy who taped Cady, and a few other dudes.

Rory's facial expression had the look of death on it. They all stopped when they saw us, and Rick had a grin on his face. I knew he was being smart, but he was fucking with the right ones when it came to us.

"Oh, what y'all can't speak?" These niggas had the nerve to be taunting us as we paid for our shit. Again, Rory isn't the talking type of nigga. He would just walk up and hit you, or should I say, knock you out and keep it moving. He felt like talking was stalling, and if you wanted to fight, there was no need to do either.

"Rory?" The dude Rick called out to him. He scoffed up a laugh and turned around with his arms folded.

"What up? It's clear you have something you wanna get off your chest." Tristan stood there silent as hell. If you didn't see him, you would've never known he was there.

"I just wanted to know how my dick tasted? I mean, I see y'all back together." Rory stood face-to-face with him. I saw the girls out the corner of my eyes running up to us. They stopped and Rick stared at Cady.

"What? You can't speak?" He was really getting under Rory's skin.

"Another time Rory. Another time." I told him and pulled him back. Cady walked straight up to Rick and smacked the shit out of him.

"Bitch, don't you ever put your hands on me." That was it. Rory hit him so hard, he was down for the count. He started stomping and kicking him in the face. Another dude went to step up, and I caught him with a two-piece that had him laid out with his friend.

"I'm coming for you, Tristan." Rory shouted.

"Fuck you, nigga. Remember, I got something you don't want seen."

"Tristan, how did it feel to see me fucking the shit out of your friend?" He sucked his teeth at Cady.

"Oh, you didn't like it? That's funny, because you're the same one who said I couldn't fuck or suck dick, but as you can see, I had you and him moaning and saying my name. So who's the bitch now?" He went to say something, but Cady stopped him.

"Rory and Miles, I don't give a fuck if you kill him. If the video gets out, so what. I don't want him having control over my fate. It's just sex; it wasn't like I was in a porno fucking different people."

"You heard her Tristan. The only reason I won't kill you right here is because we're in this mall, but you better believe, there's a bullet with your name on it."

"Whatever." He tried to sound all tough but his facial expressions showed a scared motherfucker. We dropped Cady and Rory off and went to Chanel's house. I wrapped my arms around her waist and put my chin on her shoulder.

"What's up, baby? Everything good."

"No. That stupid ex of yours tried to get me fired."

"What?" I turned her around to make sure I heard her correctly.

"Yea. Luckily, Niecy is my girl and the store manager. She said Tory came in there saying I was stealing one night she was there, and she saw me and some guy in a back office having sex."

"Well, the second part is true baby. We did fuck in your

office." I reminded her trying to lighten the mood.

"I know that fool, but how did she know? The store was closed already, unless her dumb ass was hiding inside. Who the hell knows? I'm just glad Niecy knew all about her and didn't believe a word she said, but what if it was someone else? I would've been fired. I'm about to whoop her ass again. Drive me over there, Miles."

"Cut it out. You're not fighting anyone with my baby in your stomach." She froze.

"Wwhaatt?" She started stuttering.

"You heard what I said."

"Ain't nobody pregnant. Where did you get that from?" She tried to walk away.

"Ok, so we're going to play this game? Fine."

"Chanel, when I make love to you, you're screaming like you can't handle it. You used to be a beast on top, and now, you go extra slow. Your titties are growing, and your hips are spreading. If there's no baby in your stomach, you must be eating bears to make you spread."

"Fuck you, Miles."

"When were you going to tell me?" She put her head down and stripped to get in the shower.

"I got in behind her, lifted her up, and wrapped her legs around my waist. I didn't penetrate her, even though that's what she wanted, because she kept trying to slide down.

"Nah, you gets nothing until you talk." She lifted her head from my neck.

"I just found out this morning. I took a test before you got here and tossed them in the garbage. Look Miles; I'm not trying to trap you, and I don't think either one of us are ready. I will make an appointment to terminate it tomorrow." I almost dropped her ass in the shower.

"I wish the fuck you would."

"But Miles."

"But my ass. The only appointment you better be making is to get prenatal vitamins." We finished showering and towel dried each other off. It didn't matter, because we ended up fucking right after.

****

216

I got up in the middle of the night to use the bathroom, and when I came out, I thought I smelled smoke. I know Chanel kept smoke detectors in her house, because I changed the batteries last week. I stepped in the other room, and the kitchen and living room were up in flames. I ran back in the room to get her. Why didn't the alarms go off?

"Baby, get up! Your house is on fire." She jumped out the bed and threw some clothes on. Thank goodness she had a fire escape; otherwise, we would've been burned alive. We got downstairs, and the fire trucks were already pulling up. It seemed like the fire spread quick as hell.

One of the firefighters came out afterwards and asked if either of us smoked. When we said no, he said a person from arson would come speak to us. The guy told us the fire was deliberately set outside the apartment. Someone took a paper towel with gasoline on one side and lit it. Since Chanel had rugs, it caught on quick and spread. Whoever it was must've put it out on the other side of the door, because there was no damage out there. Chanel and I both looked at each other when he walked off.

"Tory."

I can't believe this bitch, not only tried to get her fired, but burned her damn house down. Thank goodness she saved all her important papers in a fireproof safe along with pictures. Chanel talking about she about to kill her, but I told her that's for me to do.

I wouldn't let her stay at Cady's mom's house or get a hotel so I made her come live with me, which I know she's going to try and make me find her a new place, but she stuck now.

I lived in a six bedroom, three-and-a-half bath, house with plenty of space for whatever. She loved the kitchen because of all the stainless steel appliances.

"What do you want for dinner Sunday?" She asked me when I walked in.

"I don't know. Whatever you want, as long as it's cooked."

"Whatever. You know I can cook."

"I know you can, baby. That's one of the reasons I love

you." That statement took her by surprise.

"You love me?"

"Of course. Why would you think I didn't?" I asked, grabbing a piece of celery out the fridge.

"I don't know. Maybe, it's because I never heard you say it."

"I guess I'll tell you more often then." I kissed her cheek and stepped out.

Cadence

It's been a couple of weeks since the shit happened at the mall between Rory and those other guys. They have eyes all over looking for Tristan, who seemed to have disappeared. We know his uncle has him put away somewhere. I guess they thought the video was going to allow them control over Rory, but I wasn't having it. If they wanted to leak it, be my guest.

I finally moved into a three-bedroom townhouse Rory decided to buy instead of rent. The furniture was delivered yesterday, and I finally felt like I had a place of my own. I lived with Tristan off and on for a few years, but it didn't feel like this. Whenever we fought, I would go home to my parent's place. Here; my name was on everything, even though Rory purchased it.

"Hello." I answered my phone.

"What up, bitch? Let's go out for lunch." Chanel spoke into the phone.

"Ok, let me get up and get myself together." We talked

for a few more minutes and decided on Chili's as usual.

"Rory, I'm going out to eat with Chanel. Do you want me to bring you something back?" He rolled over and pulled me on top of him.

He and I have been inseparable since we got back together. Even though he has his own place, he's been over here with me. I don't mind, because he is where I wanna be.

"No, I don't want any Chili's to eat. I want something else." He kissed my lips, then my neck, and rolled me back over.

"Oh, yea? What you want to eat then?" He grinned and went down to his safe spot in between my legs.

"Mmmmm, just the way I like it. Nice and warm."

"Yes, Rory. Just like that. Suck it." He had me cumming back-to-back. He entered me nice and slow, stroking me gently. Rory always wanted to make love to me like it was his last time.

"Whose pussy is this Cady?" He had my legs lifted back behind by my head.

"It's yours, Rory, forever."

"Are you sure?"

"Yes, baby. Yes. Oh God. Right there. Here I cum, again." I squirted on his stomach.

"I love you, Rory."

"I love you too, Cady. Don't ever forget that." He started pumping harder and faster. We changed positions a few times before we both climaxed.

"That's my dick, Rory?"

"Always."

"Good. When I come back from lunch, I'm going to need some more." He laughed and grabbed my hand so we could both get in the shower.

I got to Chili's around noon, and Chanel was pulling in behind me. We sat down and placed our orders.

"Hello, Cady." I knew the voice, but didn't want to look up. I turned my head, and he was still handsome as ever.

He was wearing a blue T-shirt, some black jeans, Jordan's on his feet, and it looked like he had a fresh cut. I could feel myself getting hot from the flashbacks of us having sex.

"What you want?" Chanel rolled her eyes.

"I wanted to say, I apologize about the tape thing, but I can't get you off my mind."

"How could you tape us Rick? I was really starting to like you." He asked me to step outside with him. Chanel gave me the eye that I shouldn't, but we were in a public place, so I knew nothing would happen.

"Cady, I enjoyed every moment I spent with you, and to be honest, I never had a woman fuck me like you did." I smirked when he said that.

"Your pussy is addicting, and no matter who I fuck, her shit can't compare to yours."

"Wow! I don't know what to say."

"Cady, can we start over?"

"I have a man now."

"Oh yea, Rory." He laughed.

"I bet he can't make you cum like I can though." He whispered in my ear and I could feel my panties getting moist.

"I won't discuss how my man makes me cum."

"Can he do this?" This nigga grabbed the back of my

hair and threw his tongue down my throat. His hand slid inside my jeans, and he let his finger circle my clit. Here I was standing in between his car and another, letting him bring me to a climax.

"Shit, Rick. I'm about to…"

"Let it go, baby." My knees buckled and he pulled his fingers out and sucked all my juices off. I don't know what I was thinking, but I put my hand in his jeans and started stroking his dick. Thank goodness no one was outside or they would've saw us fondling the hell out of each other. He was getting harder by the second.

"Shit, Cady."

"You like this Rick?"

"Yea, but I'd rather be inside you. Fuck, you're about to make me cum." A few minutes later, he shot his liquid out on the ground. We stood there kissing for what seemed like forever.

"I'm not letting you go Cady, so don't get comfortable with the nigga."

"Rick, I'm not leaving him."

"We'll see about that. If I can't have you, he won't either." He got in his car to leave.

"Rick, why you acting like this?"

"I don't know what you did, but it's something about you that I can't let go. You can play house for now, but trust me when I say, you'll be mine." I put my head down to go back inside.

"Don't worry, I won't tell anyone what we just did." I sat back down, and my girl knew something was wrong. When I told her, she had this look of disgust on her face.

"Cady, all I'm going to say is be careful. I can't tell you what to do, but what you just did probably made the situation ten times worse."

"I know. I don't know what I was thinking."

"You need to tell Rory." My eyes grew big as hell when she said that.

"You need to tell him about what Rick said. I think he will kill you if he found out you let him touch you."

"I swear I won't ever let him do that again. I love Rory so much, and Rick caught me off guard. I should've stopped it, and since I didn't, I have to be woman enough to tell my man. I don't want to keep any secrets from him. And knowing the type of nigga Rick is, he'll tell anyway. I'm just going to have to face the consequences."

Rick called me over and over for the next week, and I refused to answer. He started threatening Rory to me if I didn't come see him. He was becoming obsessive over me, and I couldn't understand why. I walked in the living room and sat on Rory's lap.

"Rory, I need you to take a ride with me." He looked at me like I was crazy.

"Where to baby?" I grabbed my keys and had him follow me.

"I want you to follow my lead, and any questions, save them for later."

"What the hell is going on?" He sat in the passenger seat and lit a Black and Mild.

"Rory, I love you to death, but I messed up and this is the only way to make it right. If you leave me, I have myself to blame."

"Cady, I'm not going anywhere, and if this is about that nigga, I already know." I slammed on the brakes hard as hell.

"What you mean you know? Are we talking about the same thing?"

"I'm sure we are."

"Then tell me."

"I know you let that nigga play with your pussy in the parking lot, and in return, you jerked him off. I also know he keeps calling and texting you threatening me, if you don't fuck with him."

"How do you know all this?" He smiled and kept smoking.

I parked in the complex, picked my phone up to dial the number, and had the person come outside. Rory stepped out and pulled me in between his legs, as he leaned on the car.

"I love you Cady, but I'm not about to let you make a fool out of me either. After this is done, I better not hear about you doing another thing with anyone else, or it's over." I wrapped my hands around his neck and kissed him.

"What up, Cady?" I heard the voice behind me.

"Look Rick, what happened last week was a mistake, and I'm here to tell you it won't happen again." He snatched my hand and pulled me away from Rory. I almost shit on myself, because I knew what was about to happen.

"What the fuck are you doing?" I asked trying to break his grip.

"I told you already, if I can't have you, neither will he." He pulled a gun out his waist and pointed it at Rory. I was not jumping in front of a bullet this time. I loved my man, but that shit hurt last time.

"Do what you got to do, bro, but even in my death, she won't be with you." Rory stood there unfazed by what Rick was doing. My man was thorough as hell, and that shit was turning me on.

"Fuck you nigga. You think you tough, but I'm about to put a hot one in your ass and fuck your bitch right after." I looked at Rory, who stared at me. I smiled, already knowing what was about to happen. I mouthed the words *I love you* to him, and he said *I know*. He threw his Black and Mild on the ground and blew out the rest of the smoke.

"You ready, bae?" I nodded my head yes.

"You ready, bae?" He did the same. Rick didn't know what was going on, and that's how we wanted it. I grabbed his dick real tight and wouldn't let go. He started yelling, and grabbed me by my hair. His gun hit the ground, and I kicked it over to my man. Rory put the gun to Rick's head and pulled me away.

"Get in the car baby." I kissed him and did what he said.

I watched Rory beat Rick so bad that he was unrecognizable. He put the silencer on and put two in his forehead. The second he got in my car, a black van pulled up and made Rick disappear.

"Damn, baby. That shit made me horny."

"Well come get your dick." I slid my pants down and fucked the shit out of my man in the same parking lot he just killed a man in. We weren't worried about anyone seeing us, because it was dark, but that didn't matter either.

"Are you mad at me?" I asked him that night in the bed.

"Nah. The day I asked you to leave, I let Taylor suck

my dick, so we're even." I couldn't even say anything.

"I'm not doing this back and forth tho. If it's us, then we can't let people continue knocking us off our square. This is it." He said and wrapped his arms around me.

"Ok, baby." We both drifted off the sleep hoping to start over with no distractions.

Rory

I was driving back from the gym, when I passed Chili's and saw my girl kissing dude. I parked not too far from where they were, lit a Black and Mild and watched the fuckery that went down. It wasn't much I could say being I let Taylor give me head, so I brushed the shit off. I know her old nigga had her self-esteem at an all-time low, so any attention she was getting, she ran with it.

I stayed at my own house that night with no intentions of seeing her. She sent me a text message saying she wanted to talk, so I figured she would tell me what happened. I sat there waiting for her to tell me, but she went on and on about some baby stuff.

A few days passed, and she was in the bathroom when her phone went off. The message popped right up on the screen, and it was dude saying he would kill me and a bunch of other shit. I didn't delete the messages, but I knew she was scared to tell me about those too. Now, here we are, a week later, and I had to give that nigga a dirt bath, because he couldn't take no for an answer.

I'll be the first to admit though, Cady's pussy is top grade, and I'm pissed she let that nigga get it. However, don't get it twisted. Another nigga won't even be allowed to sniff her shit from here on out.

We had a meeting today at Donovan's house, again, and I'm sure it was about me killing Rick. He could care less, but this just made everything more complicated. I pulled up to Miles' house and waited for him to come outside.

"What's up, bro?" He said jumping in the car.

"Nothing man. What's up with you?" I passed him the mild and drove off.

"What's going on with you and Cady?"

"We cool. I just told her she better not let anyone else get close to her or its over for real."

"Ok, now what? Are you two finished fucking around on each other?"

"Yea, man. I definitely love the hell out of her. I was thinking about asking her to marry a nigga. What you think?"

"I think you have to do what's best for you, but make sure you're ready, and you're not just doing it, because you don't want her with anyone else. You know it doesn't turn out well when you do that. The marriage will be filled with nothing but regret."

"Who are you? Dr. Phil or some damn body?"

"Nah, man. I thought about asking Chanel the same thing, but I have to make sure I'm ok with being with just one woman for the rest of my life."

"Yea, I'm good with just having Cady forever. I just hope she feels the same about me. If she doesn't, oh fucking well." We both laughed and parked behind Donovan's Hummer. We stepped inside, and there were people everywhere.

"What's up, D? Why all these people here?" He led us in the room where everyone was. He introduced us to them, and they were *"Bloods"* from all over to discuss the bullshit going on with Mace and his stupid ass nephew.

"Ok, now that everyone is here, let's get down to the real reason why we're here." Donovan explained the drama, along with the fact a sex tape was made of Cady. The men in the room turned their faces up, because most of them knew her growing up and considered her their sister, so to hear that, pissed them off.

"Ok. Now that Rick is out of the equation, what are we going to do about the rest of them?" One of the guys asked.

"I say we go over there and kill all them motherfuckers. What's the use in waiting? This will give them time to come up with their own plan." I nodded my head in agreement, because I felt the same way.

"Tristan is mine. I want to be the nigga to watch him take his last breath." I told them standing up. D nodded his head and told everyone that if anyone ran across him first, bring him back alive.

The plan was for everyone to go home and chill out for a while. He would send for everyone with a time and place to meet up. Miles and I stayed back once everyone left to kick it with D.

"What's up, Rory? I know you stayed here for a reason." Donovan sat in the recliner across from me.

"Yea. I just wanted to tell you I already know where Tristan and his uncle are."

"Ok. What are you waiting for?"

"I'm making sure you're ok with being the one to tell his sister, that her brother and son will be gone before the night is over."

"I'm not worried about her. She knows the game, even though she tries to act otherwise." I gave him a pound and headed out with Miles. I dropped him off and told him I would pick him up around midnight to get rid of this stupid nigga.

I parked in my driveway and put my key in the door. When I opened it, Tristan and his uncle were sitting in my living room. I scoffed up a laugh and closed the door. These motherfuckers were bold to come in my house, but they weren't ruffling any feathers this way. I knew they were weak, because no real niggas would be this calm.

"What do I owe the pleasure of having you two idiots in my house?"

"Listen man. I just want to apologize for shooting at you and almost killing Cady." I shook my head laughing. What gang member apologizes to his arch enemy?

"It's all good. You ready to die now?" I was straight to the point with no chaser.

"Come on, Rory. He was man enough to apologize to you. Can't we get past this and move on?" Mace asked, standing in between us.

"Nah. We may have been able to do that had he not killed what would've been my first kid."

"Why does everyone keep saying that? She wasn't pregnant." His uncle spoke. Tristan put his head down like the bitch he was.

"Oh, she wasn't? Let me show you her discharge papers from the hospital." I got them out my kitchen drawer and threw them at him. I don't know why I saved them, but I wanted to show his dumb ass, because Tristan must've told him something else.

"Tristan, you didn't tell me this shit. I thought they were lying, because you swore on your mother; my sister that it wasn't true."

"Look, I'm not about to listen to you niggas bicker back and forth over what was the truth or not." I pointed the gun and let two shots off in Tristan's forehead. He hit the floor with blood leaking all over my rug. Mace put his hands up in surrender knowing he was next.

"Don't do this, Rory."

"I don t know if anyone told you, but talking isn't my forte, so say your prayers, my nigga, because it's lights out for your ass too." I let off a shot, and he fell back holding his chest. I stood over him with a smile on my face and let more shots off in his head. I'm not with that coming back to life after you been shot shit. I make sure you're dead when I do the killing. I don't need anyone coming back for revenge.

I picked my phone up and hit Donovan and Miles up and told them that the situation was handled. They got to my house in record time.

"How did you get them at the same time?" I explained to them what I came home to, as the clean-up crew disposed of their bodies and the carpet. We sat there chopping it up until the wee hours of the morning.

"Alright, I'm heading over to Cady's house before she texts me one more time threatening me." We laughed and left.

Donovan

I stepped in my office after I left Rory's house and fixed myself a drink. I was happy he took care of the situation, but I knew it wasn't over yet. His sister Patrice, had been calling me non-stop, still trying to get me to smooth things over. There was no way in hell that was going to happen, so I let her think what she wanted.

I finished up my drink, and shut all the lights off when the doorbell rang. I opened it to find Patrice on the other side with tears in her eyes. I pulled her in for a hug and noticed something was off with her but I remained quiet.

"What you doing here?" I asked offering her a seat on my couch.

"I came by because my brother and son are missing." I gave her a skeptical look. How would she know that and Rory just put them in the ground?

"Well, I haven't seen them."

"Come on Donovan. My brother was supposed to visit with Rory and try to call a truce. That was hours ago, and neither one of them are answering their phones."

"Ok. Then, if you know that much, why are you questioning me?" She wiped the tears from her eyes and stepped closer to me. She kissed my lips gently and started feeling on my dick. I pushed her back because she was married.

"Look Patrice, whatever you going through, this isn't the way to get answers." I could tell she was hurt, but I already knew what was up when she came through the door.

"Whatever, Donovan. Can you please tell me what Rory did to my brother and son?"

"Again. I don't know what you're talking about."

"I know you just got here, because I've been waiting for you, which means you probably came from being with him." That was it. She was asking too many questions and trying to get me to open my mouth. I grabbed her things and pushed her towards the door.

"Really? You're kicking me out after everything we've been through?"

"Patrice, after everything we been through, you should know I don't play when it comes to snitches or bitches trying to set a nigga up." Her eyes grew big, and she started shaking.

"What? What are you talking about?" I laughed and opened the door.

"No matter how much you tried to throw yourself at me, it won't make up for the wire you're wearing to catch me slipping." She didn't say anything.

"You see, when I hugged you, I felt it pressed against my chest, and once all the questions came, I knew you were fishing for answers to questions I don't have."

"I'm sorry, Donovan. I just wanted to find my son."

"By setting me up? Baby girl, you're lucky." I caught myself before I said anything incriminating.

"You're right; I just came back from Rory's house, and there was no one there but him, so whatever it is you're looking for, or whoever sent you here to set me up, tell them I'm not doing their job." She was speechless. I couldn't believe the dumb bitch thought she would catch me slipping. That's why I just fuck them and leave them. It's too much shit with

women. I locked up and took my ass to bed.

242

Miles

The night Rory took out Tristan and Mace, I figured there would be no more problems, but I was wrong. It seemed like niggas from the *"Crips"* were trying to get at anyone affiliated with us, assuming we were the ones for their disappearance. It doesn't matter that we were, but they didn't know that shit.

We had to take extra precaution, until we found out who this new dude is coming in tryna take over Mace's position. We heard he was some dude from New York who was next in line to run shit, but we have yet to cross paths.

Chanel and I were pulling into Perkins when she stopped short making my weed fall out the blunt. I looked at her, and she had a smirk on her face. When I saw what she was looking at, I did the same. Tory was walking to her car by herself and must've dropped something.

"Run her ass over if you want." I told her, and my body jerked as she did just that. By the time my ex realized what happened, Chanel ran her ass over.

"Oh, shit. You really did it. Girl, you crazy, but I love you." I kissed her, and we both stepped out the car. People started coming out of the restaurant looking and on their phones probably calling the cops.

"Bitch, you did that shit on purpose." Tory screamed out with tears rolling down her face. Chanel said she didn't wanna kill her, but made sure she would leave a permanent mark on her, and I think she did.

Tory's leg was turned in the opposite direction with the bone popped out. Her other leg seemed to have suffered some damage too, because there was blood pouring out.

"Are you ok, Ma'am?" Chanel asked her in a polite way.

"Chanel, fuck you. I know you did this on purpose." I saw people looking and trying to listen.

"Back up everyone, so the ambulance can get through."

"Bitch, the next time you won't survive. Now, be a nice little girl and tell them you weren't paying attention and walked out in front of me. If you say otherwise, I will come to that hospital, and it's lights out for you." I told her.

"Why are you doing this?"

"I told you to leave her the fuck alone, and you kept fucking with her."

"You're going to take her side after she did this?" I glanced around to see how many people were paying attention to her theatrics.

"Tory, did you hear what I said?"

"Yes. I walked out in front of her. I know."

"Good. You should be happy you're still alive. If it was me, I would've dragged you under my car, down the street just to make sure you were dead. Peace out, bitch." Chanel didn't even blink an eye or seem shaken up. My baby was handling this shit like it was nothing.

After the cops questioned us for about twenty minutes, we went in and had lunch.

****

"Baby, what did you say to her to make her change her story?"

"It doesn't matter. Just know she won't be bothering you anymore." I told her, kissing on her neck. I made love to her for a few hours, and then left the house. I had to make sure Tory's dumb ass wasn't talking. I got to the hospital and found out what room she was in. There were two dudes sitting inside talking to her, so I stayed outside listening to what he was saying.

"Tory, you sure this was an accident? I mean, who drives fast in a parking lot?"

"I didn't say she was driving fast. I wasn't paying attention, ok. Damn, I'm the one fucked up in here, and you treating me like I did this to myself."

"Alright, my bad. I'm just watching out for you sis."

Sis. I didn't know this bitch had brothers, and I've been with her for a minute. I waited down the hall for them to leave and walked in. She was shocked and grabbed the nurse's button, but I removed it from her hand.

"Girl, chill out. If I wanted to finish the job, you wouldn't have been able to reach for the button." She stared at me and then, started to relax.

"Miles, why did you let this happen?" I closed the door before I spoke.

"You did this to yourself, Tory."

"Ugh, I beg to differ."

"You should've left well enough alone when I told you to. I don't get why you even care if I'm with someone else. I mean, why did you think it was ok for you to burn her house down or try to get her fired?"

"I just wanted you back." I saw the tears escaping her eyes. I didn't have one bit of compassion for her sneaky ass.

"Who were those niggas in here?"

"That's just my brother and his friend." She waved her hand off.

"When did you get a brother? I've never heard you talk about him, and I damn sure ain't never seen him."

"He's my brother on my dad's side. We don't really fuck with each other like that. He came to town to take over some niggas spot who went missing."

"Wait! He did what?" She started telling me the reason he was here, and that if the two men didn't show up soon, there will be bloodshed all through the city and some other shit I wasn't listening to.

All I could think of was, not only is he the man to take Mace's spot, but he's a rival gang member with his own army. I sent Rory and D a text saying we had to meet up ASAP.

I reminded Tory of what I told her and chucked up the deuces before I left. I went back out, through the emergency department, since that was the way I came in, when I noticed an ambulance taking the stretcher out the back. I looked down, and it was Taylor. She was in bad shape.

"Excuse me. What happened to her?" I asked the EMT.

"Are you related to her?"

"No, she's just a friend."

"I can't give you any information on her, but if you know her family, can you contact them and tell them to get down here quick?" He and his partner went through the automatic doors, and I watched them rush her to the back. I had to send Rory a different text.

    Me: *Change of plans, bro. You need to meet me at the emergency room right now.*

Rory

I was getting dressed when Cady told me my phone went off again, and it was a message telling me to get to the hospital. When I told her what the message said, she jumped up to get dressed herself. Miles didn't say what happened, but I'm sure she assumed it was Chanel, especially since she wasn't answering her phone.

We parked in the section of the emergency room and went inside. Miles began telling us what he saw and what the EMT told us. I wasn't sure where her parents were, because they were always on vacation somewhere. I told the lady at the front desk I was her husband, and since we still had the same last name, she had no choice but to believe me.

"The doctor will be out to see you soon, Mr. Rogers." The lady at the receptionist desk told me.

"Baby. You don't have to stay here if you don't want to. I know you're tired."

"It's ok. I wanna make sure the baby is ok. They are going to be related." I kissed her on the forehead, because I didn't want the receptionist to question anything. The doctor came out an hour or so later and came to sit by me.

"I'm sorry Mr. Rogers, but your wife didn't make it." I know I should be hurt, but I really wasn't. Miles and Cady looked at me for some sign that I would break down but there was none.

"What happened to her?"

"She was hit by a drunk driver. Well, that's what the EMT's told us. When they arrived on the scene, the other driver had a gash on his forehead and was so intoxicated, he couldn't walk."

"What about the baby?"

"What baby? Was there a baby in the car with her?"

"No. She was pregnant. She should've been four months." I only knew that, because her and Cady were the same.

"Mrs. Rogers wasn't pregnant."

"WHAT????"

"I'm sorry. Were you informed that she was?" He asked, with a confused look on his face.

"Are you sure she wasn't with child? She told me she was pregnant."

"I'm sorry you were misinformed, but Mrs. Rogers couldn't have kids. She had a hysterectomy when she was twenty years old."

"Huh?"

"I remember her coming into the emergency room with bad stomach pains. When we checked her out, she had Uterine Prolapse. This is a benign condition in which the uterus moves from its usual place down into the vagina. I'm sorry that she never told you she had it."

I thought back to when she could have gotten it, and it had to be when I was locked up. I can't believe the bitch never told me. Whether I chose to have kids with her or not, she still should've told me.

"She showed me an ultrasound picture. How did she get it if she wasn't?"

"Sir, you can get anything off the internet. Did you check the name at the top of it? When a woman gets one, her information is logged into the computer, and when the picture is taken, it's all on the photo."

"I never even thought to look at it. I just assumed she was telling the truth." He patted me on my back and gave me his condolences again before leaving.

"Are you ok baby?" Cadence sat on my lap. I didn't care who was looking at this point. This bitch played me too many times, and even in her death, she made a fool of me.

"Yea, I'm good. At least I know this baby is real." I told her rubbing her stomach. I stood up, and we all went to walk out.

"Mr. Rogers, do you want to say any final goodbyes to her before you leave?" The receptionist asked.

"Nah. Fuck that bitch." The look on her face was priceless, along with the other nosey people sitting in there.

I called her mom's phone, but it went to voicemail. I left her ass a messgae telling her to get to the hospital. I was done with that family now and forever. The only person I was focused on was Cady and my unborn child. At this point nothing else mattered.

Cadence

I felt bad for Rory when we left the hospital. He may not have wanted a child with Taylor, but the way she tricked him into believing she was expecting is foul.

We got back to my house and saw my front door opened. I know damn well I didn't leave it that way. Rory sat back in the driver seat in deep thought. I wasn't going to say anything, because when he was like this, I knew nothing good was about to come out of it.

"Baby, call your uncle and tell him you're on the way over there, and that it's time."

"HELL NO!!! I'm not leaving you." I yelled out. He smiled and blew smoke out.

"Cadence, now is not the time for you to throw a tantrum. I need you to trust me on this." I called my uncle and told him what Rory said.

"He told me to wait here, and he would be by to get me. He doesn't want me to drive without some sort of escort from someone." I hung the phone up and looked at him.

"What's about to happen?"

"You know I'm not gonna tell you. The less you know, the better baby." He leaned down and kissed me passionately. The kiss felt like I would never get another one. I didn't want to stop, but he pulled back and opened his car door, when he saw headlights coming in the driveway. The cars stopped and before we could step out, bullets were flying everywhere.

Rory pulled my body down and covered me with his the best he could. When it stopped, I felt my body being lifted out. I was kicking and screaming until I heard my uncle yelling in my ear to calm down. I glanced over at Rory, and he was still hunched over in the front seat.

"Put me down." I screamed and ran over to him. He had blood coming from his mouth, and his shirt was full of blood.

"Rory get up baby. Please." I was hysterical as they put him in a truck. I jumped in with them and laid his head down on my lap.

"Hurry up. Please don't die, Rory." He started coughing up blood, so I rolled him over on his side so he wouldn't choke on it.

"We're almost there Cadence. Keep talking to him. He can hear you, even though he can't respond." My uncle said driving and looking back.

"Rory, I love you so much. Stay with me. You have to make it, so you can be here for the baby. Baby, please." I felt him grab my hand and try to squeeze it. I knew he heard me and was trying to hold on.

"Ok, we're here. Cadence, run in and tell them your boyfriend was shot and you need help."

"I can't leave him. Can't you do it?"

"Cady, I know you're scared, but we can't be here. Now, GET OUT AND GO GET HELP." He yelled at me.

I laid Rory's head on the seat and went in screaming. Doctor's came out with a stretcher and took him in the back.

My uncle pulled off in another car and told me to call him when I hear something. I parked the car and ran back inside and waited for what seemed like forever. I had to keep calm, because I know this was stressing the hell out of my baby. I tried to call Chanel, and she still wasn't answering, so I dialed Miles' number, and he answered on the third ring.

"Cady, please tell me Chanel is with you."

"What do you mean? I've been calling her all night, and she hasn't been answering. I thought she was with you."

"No. I went home after we left the hospital, and she wasn't here. I assumed she was on her way to your house or her mom's since the car was gone. She's not answering her phone."

"I'm sure she's ok, Miles. Her phone probably died. Listen, I need you to get back to the hospital right away."

"Why? What happened?" He asked.

"Rory has been shot and -?" I didn't finish my sentence when I saw the home screen on my phone pop up. I can't believe this nigga hung up on me. Rory's parents came in after I hung up with Miles.

"Oh, my God Cady. Is he ok?" His mom asked squeezing me. I'm sure my uncle called them.

"I don't know. They're working on him right now." They both sat on each side of me while we waited for the doctor and Miles.

"What's taking Miles so long?" His dad wanted to know.

"I don't know. This isn't like him." We were all starting to get worried, because they were like brothers. There was no way in hell Miles wouldn't be here.

The doctor stepped out and asked to speak to his parents. They told him, I could stay and he could speak freely with me being there.

"Rory was shot in his abdomen and back." I covered my mouth and gasped.

"He's going to be ok, and he will not be paralyzed before you ask. The bullet missed his spine by a few inches. He was very lucky."

"Can we go see him?"

"Yes. He should be in a room within the hour. Just remember, he's on pain medicine, so he may or may not be awake when you get there." He shook all of our hands and left. I sent a message to my uncle that he was ok, but that detectives were lurking around of course.

He called me on the phone and told me something else was going down, because Miles told him Chanel was missing, and that after they cleaned up my house, he went to get Miles, and his car door was open, but he wasn't in it.

"Shit." Rory's parents both looked at me in shock. I hung the phone up and took a deep breath.

"What's wrong Cadence?" His dad asked.

"Miles and Chanel are missing." He hopped up out of that seat so quick, I thought there was a fire under his ass.

"What do you mean missing?" The bass in his voice had me nervous.

"I'm not sure of everything, but he said all this was a setup. As far as Rory getting shot and Miles and Chanel missing. Oh my God, she's pregnan, too. We have to find them." I was starting to cry, and his mom pulled me in for a hug.

"Cady, you stay here with my wife and wait to go see my son. Do not leave his side; either one of you. Do you understand?" We both nodded our heads. They walked outside, and I saw her arguing with him. He kissed her and walked off in the direction of his car. She came in wiping her eyes just as the nurse came out to get us to go in.

✳✳✳✳✳✳✳✳✳✳✳✳✳✳✳✳✳✳✳✳✳✳✳✳✳

"Hey baby." He whispered out. I ran over to him and kissed his lips. He had machines hooked up to him, but he still grabbed me and made me sit on the bed with him. I got in as carefully as I could not to cause any pain.

"Are you ok?"

"You know they can't kill me. I wasn't leaving you or my baby." He kissed my tears that wouldn't stop falling. He rubbed my stomach the best he could and smiled.

"Come here, Ma." She kissed his forehead.

"Rory, I thought we lost you." He pressed the button for the bed to raise up.

"Ma, you know I wouldn't leave you or Pops either. Matter of fact, where is he?" She and I glanced at one another.

"Do you want something to drink baby?" She asked him reaching for the pitcher on his tray table.

"Don't change the subject. Yo, where is Pops and Miles?" I could tell he was getting aggravated. The heart machine started going off, and a nurse came in.

"Is everything ok?" She asked, smiling in his face.

"Nah, I'm good. My wife and mom won't give me information; that's all." I saw her face turn up when he said wife. That's what her ass gets for trying to pick up a man that's been shot. I swear some women have no shame. When she left, Rory went back to the same question he asked previously.

"Your dad is with Donovan."

"Ok, why isn't he here? And where the fuck is Miles?"

"Your dad was here, but he had to leave."

"Ok. It better be that fucking important he had to leave his son in the hospital." I guess his mom felt bad, because it did look suspect, but when she told him Miles was missing, he almost lost it. He snatched the IV out his arm, and all the monitor plugs off his chest, and anywhere else they were.

"Rory, what are you doing?" He was trying to get out the bed but could barely move. The nurse came back in with a shocked look.

"Mr. Rogers why did you disconnect yourself? You need to rest."

"Nah. Do me a favor and get my discharge papers. Fuck that; I'm leaving."

"Sir, I don't think that's a good idea. Let me get the doctor." She ran out, and you could hear her paging the doctor.

"Rory, where are you going? You are not well." His mom said but helping him put his clothes on. I sat there watching him fight through his pain to go find his brother from another mother.

"Let's go." I hopped off the bed, and he used me and his mom's shoulders to hold him up. We left the hospital in such a rush, you would've thought someone died.

"Text your uncle right now, and ask him where he is, and if he knows where Miles and Chanel are?" I let him lay on my lap while his mom drove to nowhere in particular. My uncle wouldn't tell me at first, but I told him I wanted to go home and stay away from whatever area they were in. He gave me an address to where they were holding Miles.

Rory wanted a ride to his house. He had me go in and gave me a code to some safe he had installed in his bedroom wall. He had a shitload of guns inside and had me bring them out.

"Rory what do you need this for?"

"Don't worry about that. These niggas want war; that's what they're about to get." He put a silencer on a gun and then, winced over in pain.

"Rory, let them handle this please. You're not well, enough." He ignored me and opened the door to the address. His adrenaline must've been pumping, because he got out the car as if he hadn't been shot hours ago. I saw the blood leaking from inside his shirt, which means he probably busted the stitches open.

"Cadence, you and my mom stay in the car. If you notice anything funny or someone comes to this car, light their ass up."

"Rory be careful. I love you."

"I love you too, Cadence. I love you, Ma." I watched him slowly disappear in the darkness.

Chanel

I knew this bitch was crazy, but I didn't know she was crazy enough to have me kidnapped. I mean, was she really that obsessed over Miles, or was this a game for her? Shit, she was already with my ex, whose dumb ass was sitting over in the corner with her rubbing her shoulders. She was grinning from ear-to-ear as he did it. I guess she thought I cared but I been over Mike.

"How does it feel to have the bitch you tried to kill, about to kill you?" Tory taunted.

"It doesn't feel like shit. If I wanted to kill you, trust and believe, you wouldn't be here."

"Oh, you're a cocky bitch. Let's see how cocky you are when my brother gets back with your man." I refused to show an ounce of fear, so I shrugged my shoulders like I didn't care.

"Damn, Chanel you looking good." Mike said, walking over to me grinning.

"No the fuck you didn't Mike. I'm sitting over here, and you're all in that bitch face. I thought you said you couldn't stand her."

"I never said that. I said she broke my heart when she left me, but seeing her has a nigga in his feelings." He licked his lips and kneeled down in front of me.

"I never meant to hurt you Chanel. She was community pussy, and I fucked up when you caught me. Can you ever forgive me for hurting you?" He looked sincere.

"I forgive you Mike, but what I can't forgive is how you allowed her to convince you to do this to me."

"I didn't convince her to do shit. I'm stuck in this just like you."

"What do you mean?"

"She came to me with a proposition to make some extra money. Now, you know I gets my own paper, but I thought what the hell. She said we were picking some chick up that her man was beefing with her brother. The money was good, so I agreed. When we got to your mom's house, I cursed her the fuck out. I went to back out, but her brother and goons had my back up against the wall. They had my son; our son, with a gun to his head." My mouth dropped to the floor when he said that.

"Excuse me. What do you mean our son?" I had no idea what he was talking about. I didn't have any kids.

"Chanel, you do have a son."

"I don't have any kids, Mike." He took his phone out and showed me a photo of a little boy who could be no older that two or three. He looked just like him but that doesn't mean he was mine.

"Chanel, do you remember when you were eight months pregnant by me, and you had the accident?" I nodded my head yes.

"Well, I paid the doctor and nurses a ton of money to tell you the baby died." The tears that left my eyes could've filled up a bucket.

"Why? Why would you do that?" I saw Tory sitting in the back grinning.

"Chanel, it's not what you think. I had to do what was in the best interest of our son." I was tied to a chair so I couldn't smack, punch, kick, or even kill him.

"How is it not what I think?"

"Chanel, I met Tory long before you. When I found out you were pregnant, I broke it off with her. I planned on making you my wife, and we were leaving this town. Unfortunately, she found out about your pregnancy and made me a promise, that she would kill the baby or have it killed, if it survived. I couldn't have that. You or my son didn't deserve that."

"What?"

"I had someone cause the accident, but they weren't trying to kill you; just make you go into labor. I'm so sorry, Chanel. I never meant to hurt you, but at the time, it was the best thing for him."

"As mad as I am, I understand." I know I shocked him when I said that, but if the deranged bitch was going to kill him, then it was for the best.

"Does he know who I am? Can I see him?" I was running question for question with him.

"That's the thing, Chanel. They have him. The only reason I'm here is to make sure he's safe."

"Who has him?"

"Her brother and his goons."

"Oh, my God. How did they find him? Where was he?"

"He was with my mom down in North Carolina. They told my mom I was in a terrible accident, and she needed to get here quick. When they picked her up from the airport, they snatched them both up. I'm trying to get Tory to tell me where he has them, but she won't unless I fuck her, and I don't want to." I gave him the side eye.

"I'm serious. I met someone, and I am really trying to make it work with us, but Tory isn't allowing that to happen." The door opened with two guys holding Miles, and within the hour, there had to be at least fifty niggas inside. This was not going to end well for any of us, and to think, I didn't get a chance to meet my son, or my unborn.

Miles

I remembered being on the phone with Cadence telling me that my brother was shot. The next thing I know, I'm in the trunk of some car. I could hear some dudes talking about how they were going to kill all of us. I never understood why people felt the need to kidnap someone if the plans were to murk them anyway. Why go through all the trouble when it could be done faster?

The car stopped and the trunk popped open. I wasn't tied up or anything, and I refused to run, because I knew Chanel was somewhere close. I couldn't let them kill her; especially with my kid in her stomach.

They grabbed me out the trunk and led me into some warehouse. I saw Chanel tied up in a chair, and Tory sitting in a wheelchair. My baby really fucked her ass up, and I could care less.

A few minutes later, more niggas piled inside with a tiny kid. I didn't know who he belonged to, but I sure as hell was shocked they brought him.

"Ok, my niggas. Here we have this bitch ass nigga who had his girl run my sister over with her car to try and kill her. Oh, and let's not forget, he's friends with the nigga that made Tristan, Rick and Mace disappear." Some nigga named Josh spoke.

"Those were some bitch ass niggas who are better off missing." I spoke up not worrying about repercussions.

"Miles. Don't antagonize them." Chanel yelled from across the room.

"Nah, baby. They should hear the dumb shit those niggas did, and why they met their fate early." I told them what happened, and each one seemed to be in cahoots with the fact they deserved to die after the disrespect, but when I started telling him about the shit his sister did, the guy Josh stopped me. He probably didn't want them to know how crazy her ass really was.

"It doesn't matter what my sister did. The shit your girl did was disrespectful, and for that, she has to die."

"Mike, tell my son I love him." She said, with tears coming down her face. *Her son.*

I saw some dude standing behind her with a gun to the back of her head, then, I saw a shadow at one of the windows and noticed Donovan looking at me. I was about to react, but the red light on dude's forehead told me not to move. He was hit by some gun that, the dude Mike had. No one knew where the shot came from, because he had a silencer on the gun and snatched the kid up and left. They were so busy scrambling for cover, I ran over to untie Chanel. I couldn't get her out quick enough before it became a war zone.

I saw a door open, and it was Chanel's ex motioning for us to come that way. I sent her to him, and he slid me a gun. I don't know why I trusted him with her, but right now, I couldn't worry about that.

"Miles come on. Baby, please." I heard her screaming.

"Get her out of here." He pulled her, but she was fighting him. He grabbed her up, and the door closed. I thought

I saw Rory inside, but I had to be bugging, because Cady told me he was shot.

There were bodies spread out all over the floor. I turned around and saw my *"Blood"* brothers standing over Josh and Tory who were in a different room.

"Well, well what do we have here?" I said.

"We have this bitch ass nigga who tried to kill me." I turned around, and Rory was barely standing up. He had bloody t-shirt on.

"Yo, you alright? Did you get hit?"

"Nah. My shit has been bleeding since I left the hospital. I had to make sure everyone was ok. I couldn't have my brothers out here risking their lives for me, and I'm lying in the hospital."

"Nigga, they know you were shot."

"It's only right that I take out the nigga, who tried to take me out." He shot Josh between the eyes, and I followed suit by doing the same with Tory. I was happy this shit was finally over.

Me and some of the other guys carried Rory outside to the car and told Cadence and his mom to take him back to the hospital, and if he decides to leave again, call one of us.

I found Chanel and Mike standing in front of a car, and to me, they were a little too close.

"Chanel." I yelled her name out, and she was smiling. I was fuming, because I know she wasn't all in this nigga's face, and I just saved her ass.

Then, I saw a little kid jumping on the car holding her hand. I wrapped my arms around her waist and waited for her to explain. When she told me that was her son, I was a little sad, because I thought she would only have my kids.

"Listen Miles. I know this is a fucked up situation, and this is new, but we do have a kid together. I don't want any animosity between us. This is about my son."

"I agree." We shook hands and gave each other a half hug.

"Oh. Congratulations on the baby." He said, walking off with Mike Jr.

"Baby, why didn't you let him come home with us?"

"I think he should stay with Mike for right now. That's the only person he knows. I don't want to rip him away from what he knows."

"Whatever you decide. You know I got your back."

"I know."

"Does he know you?"

"Yes. He calls me mommy. Mike has shown him pictures of me. He said, he knew there would come a day where he would bring him back to me."

"Everything happens for a reason baby. This was the ending of a new beginning for you. You have your son, my seed, and me. What else do you need?" She smiled and grabbed my dick.

"I need some of this."

"Oh, yea. Well, he needs you, too. Come on, so I can eat before I go to bed." I picked her up and carried her to Donovan's car.

"Baby, I'm happy you saved me. I found out I had a son, and now, all the drama is over."

"When am I going to meet him? You know he's about to be in football right?" I told her.

"I'm going to get him on the weekends to start, and then, we'll share custody. He has a baby on the way, too, so Mike Jr. will be a big brother twice. And football? I don't know."

"Girl, please. He's not going to be a momma's boy. That's our little superstar."

Rory

Cadence and my mom brought me back to the hospital, and the doctors act like they were happy to see me. They put out one of those Silver Alerts all over. It's almost like the Amber alert for a kid, but instead, it's for adults who leave the hospital without being discharged and could be in danger. They had housekeeping clean my room, and the nurses hooked me back up to the machines.

"Can you guys excuse us so I can give Mr. Rogers a sponge bath?" I thought Cadence was going to slap the shit out of her.

"Ugh, no we cannot. And let this be the last time I say this to you. The only woman washing my man's dick is me. If I find out you even peeked at his shit, you can believe I will report your ass." Her face turned beet red. There was nothing she could do but leave.

"Baby, why you do that? You know I have to wash."

"Yea ok, Rory. I'll wash your ass if that's the case."
My mom was cracking up.

"Ma, how are you going to sit over there laughing?"

"Boy, I would've done the same thing if it was your
father. She was being disrespectful so that's what her ass gets.
You told her she was your wife and she still tried it."

"That's my dick. Don't get a bitch fucked up trying to
get a sneak peek." She whispered in my ear. I laid back with
her on my bed. I didn't realize I fell asleep until I woke up the
next afternoon.

Cadence was still by my side, but she had different
clothes on. Miles had Chanel on his lap, and my Pops and
Donovan were in the corner talking and laughing. My room
was filled with so many people, we had to close the door,
because people were complaining about the noise.

"Cady can you take me in the bathroom to wash up?"
Miles helped me walk in the bathroom. There was a seat in the
shower that I had him sit me on. I wasn't supposed to take a
shower, but this sponge bath shit didn't make me feel clean
enough. Cady came in with my clothes and hygiene products.

"I love you, Cady." I told her, as she washed me up. She took her time trying not to hurt me.

"I love you too, Rory." She kissed my lips and continued. When she washed my dick, he sprung to life for her.

"Well. It looks like someone needs me to talk to him." She smiled and licked her lips.

"It's ok baby. I can wait."

"Yea, but he can't." She turned the shower head to the side and spoke in the microphone. She had me moaning like a bitch so bad, I know everyone heard me. She swallowed every one of my kids.

"Let me please you."

"No. I'm ok." I grabbed her by the waist and unbuttoned her pants. Instead of fighting, she gave me what I wanted. I had her turn around so I could eat her from the back. She had back-to-back orgasms in my mouth, and I cleaned her up with my tongue.

Instead of stopping, she slid down and rode me until we both climaxed at the same time. She ended up washing both of us up. After we got dressed, she called Miles back in to help me back in the room.

"Damn, y'all couldn't wait until you got home?" Chanel asked Cady when we walked out.

"What? My man needed it, and who am I to tell him no?" I laughed and gave Miles a look.

"Come here, Cady." She turned around and stood in front of me.

"Baby, I can't get down on one knee, but I can't go another day without asking you to spend the rest of your life with me. What plans do you have for the future, because if you don't have any, I want it to be with me? Will you marry me?" She had tears falling down her face, as she nodded her head yes.

Miles passed me the ring. It was a 10-carat canary yellow diamond from Tiffany's. I know she didn't expect something so big, but I told her I would give her the world, and I meant it.

"Congratulations." Chanel said, giving her a hug and more followed. I saw Miles get on his knee in front of Chanel.

I pulled Cady close to me and watched him confess his love to her. Chanel was crying harder than Cady; especially when she saw we picked out the same rings for them. Those two were thick as thieves like Miles and I were, so it was no question they would love the same thing.

"Baby, thank you for everything." Cady said kissing my lips.

"You're welcome."

"We both ended up with scars, but the love we had for one another helped us move past them and I can't wait to be your wife."

"And I can't wait to be your husband."

THE END!!!